WALKING CONTRADICTION

R. LATICE

ISBN: 978-1-7350557-0-1 (Paperback)

Cover Illustrations by: Will Nika Draw.
(Instagram-@will_nika_draw_)
Cover Design by: Kenon Givens.
Published by: Ward's Publishing House

First printing edition 2020.

Ward's Publishing House
wardspublishinghouse@gmail.com
Little Rock, AR

www.rlatice.com
www.wardspublishinghouse.com

To all the eyes that read this book, you are my first supporters. I can never thank you enough, but I'll say thank you every chance I get. Thank you!

...Who am I?
Prompts that panic attack feeling.
Quickened heartbeat, feeling of lost control.
Unable to discern what's real
Who I am...
I mean, who am I?
The specifics are blurry.
Truth is,
The pilots change.
I'm on auto pilot so much,
I hardly remember.

-R. Latice

Prologue

"Ryan, wake up girl. Wake up!" an unfamiliar voice shouts. It sounds as if she's screaming from a tunnel. I feel someone shaking me hard as my eyes begin to roll open slowly. I feel groggy, and everything around me is foreign. I see a tall, skinny, light-skinned woman, who appears to be Latina, hovering over my body. She has a slight accent, almost non-existent to the point that she sounds like she was raised in the US her entire life.

She's gorgeous with big beautiful hazel eyes, plump lips, and has a crooked narrow nose, so it throws her features off a bit. A look of concern is plastered across her face. Her eyes are red; I'd assume she's been crying a little. I've never seen her a day in my life. And who the fuck is Ryan?

"I'm sorry. Who are you?" I manage to utter, dazed out of my mind.

"Ryan, stop playing. Are you ok girl? You kinda just passed out".

I pull myself up from the cold, dusty floor. I begin to feel around for my purse. I see it at my feet and grab it quickly, ravaging through it until I find my compact mirror. I pull it out and get lost in my reflection for a while. Nope, still the same face. I look the same. My big luscious lips are glossed to perfection. My natural hair is in its usual fluffy wash and go, and my new highlights of honey blonde are setting off my brown hair. The color makes my light brown, almond-shaped eyes pop against my brown skin more than usual.

My makeup is the only thing that appears to be out of the ordinary. It's a little dramatic for my taste, but I'm still me. Thank God. I let out a big sigh of relief. I can't understand why she's calling me a different name than my own. My first thought is that I must look like someone she knows. I don't have the energy for this right now, my head is killing me, and I can't remember a thing.

"My name is not Ryan. I'm Koni. I'm sorry."

"Girl, who the fuck is Koni? I've been with you all night like we are every night that you come in here! Hello, get a grip, you tripping. I think I need to call a doctor because it sounds like yo' ass got a concussion on the way down. Hang tight girl. I'll be right back," she walks away towards the entrance.

A beautiful, god of a man, enters the establishment; caramel skin, built like he lifts thick women like me for a living. I can't help but stare at him. His deep waves embedded in his fresh fade, showcase his excellent grade of naturally curly hair. He has the prettiest smile. I notice he has a dimple from way back here, only on his left side. The woman walks to him as soon as he walks in, she leans in to whisper something in his ear and begins to point in my direction. He starts to walk toward me.

"See if you can get her to remember who she is, Gabe!" she yells with panic in her voice as she rushes away with her phone in her hand.

A slight accent is developing with a heightened sense of fear in her voice. Now, I'm really confused. All night? What the hell is she talking about? I don't even know her; I definitely don't go hanging out with strangers. I would usually be passed out in my bed by now. Come to think of it, the last thing I really remember from tonight is taking the medicine that usually knocks me out cold. Klonapin. My doctor prescribed it for anxiety, but it also helps me sleep.

Looking around the room, I don't even know where I am exactly. It appears to be a bar. It feels eerily familiar, but nothing stands out to me. Nothing about this seems like my type of scene. Everyone is looking at me. I can't find a recognizable face. They don't even look like the type of people I'd hang around. It is a diverse crowd but still strange. All of them look like they came from either the country or the slums. I can't lie; it's all a little threatening. I get off the floor and begin to straighten and dust off my dress. The man is now standing in my face.

"Ryan, what the fuck? You drunk or something? Rocky over there saying you acting weird and shit. You good baby?" He places his hand on my back.

Baby? Something about him seems familiar too. Not appearance-wise, but I can almost feel a connection to him, even with this being my first time encountering him. I know I'd remember meeting a man this fine. For a second, I almost forget about my man. I instantly wish I were with him instead. The woman is talking on the phone, arranging an ambulance to come to pick me up, although she keeps calling me Ryan. I overhear a male next to her call her Raquel but everyone else refers to her as Rocky.

"My name is Koni. I'm sorry. Y'all have me confused

with someone else. I don't mean any harm, but I can't even remember how I got here. I think I should go home now. It was nice to meet you all! Sorry about the misunderstanding." I get myself together and begin to head towards the door.

Now, Rocky is off the phone. They both instantly try to stop me from leaving by blocking my way. I'm supposed to be in bed, and my head is spinning. I dig into my purse, pull my license from my wallet, and glance over it, expecting it to say someone else's name the way they're acting. They almost had me convinced that it would.

"Ok. I don't know what's going on, but I need to get home. I have to work in a few hours. I'm not going to worry myself with the questions, but I can tell you without a shadow of a doubt that my name is Koni. And just to stop all the extra, here is my license." I hand over my license, annoyed.

I don't know what's going on. I start to think that maybe I got blackout drunk. I've done that a few times. Friends would tell me about it later, and none of it ever sounded familiar. But this is extreme compared to those times. I watch them dissect my license, steadily looking up at me and back down to the license. They both look just as confused as I am about being here.

"Girl, what the fuck kinda shit you got going? Why you tell us it was Ryan this whole time?' Rocky says, now with a rougher almost hood accent. She looks over at the man and shakes her head. He isn't saying a word, just standing there zoned out. 'Then, obviously, Gabe doesn't know it either. And y'all been fucking for two years! This shit is crazy."

I have to get away from here. My mind is in overdrive

trying to make sense of it all. I have never seen her or this man in my life. Fucking? I'd never cheat on Xavier. Even with this fine ass man.

"Why are you looking like that? Unless you're a twin? Do you have a twin? What'd you say the name was, Kori?" she says sarcastically.

"It's Koni. And no, I don't have a twin. I'm an only child. I don't have any siblings. How did I even get here?"

"Girl, you are blowing my fucking high. Are you higher than me? Because, bitch, you sounding real crazy right now. Shit, did you do something other than weed? You got here the same fucking way you always do, look at your car outside. Fuck girl, you are really starting to worry me."

Gabe reaches out and gently grabs both of my arms as he stares into my eyes. "Ry, what's going on, baby? Is this a fake I.D? You on that shit or something?"

"Sir, let me the fuck go.' I snatch my arms away from him. "For the last time, my name is Koni! Damn, what aren't y'all getting? Shit, I'm starting to think I have a twin my damn self. And I know damn well I don't. You people are crazy. I don't even know y'all, and I refuse to let y'all sit here and play with my head like this. Now, I'm going home, so please both of you, get the fuck out of my way." I storm out.

I hate having to get ignorant and hate causing a scene even more. By the time I make it to my car, Gabe rushes out and snatches my keys.

"You ain't going nowhere like this. You really need to go to a doctor because you outta whack. I think you knocked something loose when you hit the damn floor." he says it slowly as if I was having a hard time comprehending. 'I scheduled you a Lyft; it will be here in two minutes. So just sit down and try to remember. I need you to think because I can't lose you again, Ry." He leans in and pulls me in tight.

Again? I snatch away. I don't feel drunk, but I'm starting to think that I just may be, that or I'm dreaming. He took my keys, and I can't find my phone, so I hope it's at home. My best bet to get home is to sit and wait. No other words are spoken until the Lyft arrives. He walks me to the back of the car and opens the door. He leans in to kiss me, and before I could catch myself, I whirl back and slap him as hard as I can.

He falls back onto the curb. I hear my keys as they hit the pavement. I grab them, hop in the Lyft, and yell, "Drive !" The driver speeds off, and I watch as Gabe gets off the ground. I can see his arms waving to try to flag us down, but the driver just keeps going.

"Looks like you've had a rough night beautiful. Are you ok?" he pries in an African accent.

"Yes," I assure, knowing I am far from it. I glance out the window, taking note of every building name I can remember. The area looks like it is downtown with the surrounding large buildings, but I've never been on this side of town before. I start to question whether my parents left a piece of my history out because if those people were acting, each one of them deserves a damn Oscar. They know me. I can feel it, but I can't pinpoint how. I wreck my mind going over old jobs, schools, previous clients, and any and everything to try to place them in my life. I come up with nothing - not one single thing. However, this wouldn't be the first time my memory has failed me.

"Ok, we're here. I hope your night gets better. That same man has scheduled me for three different women in the last week. So, don't be embarrassed. Just stay beautiful."

From his comment, I begin to think this is a game for them, like they were just fucking with me. I'm even wondering if it was an attempt to trick me into sex trafficking or something. I always overthink and go for the extremes. I get out of my head long enough to thank the driver for getting me home safe. I let him know how appreciative I am that he pulled off when I asked and how I'm going to let it reflect in my tip in the app when I get upstairs to my phone.

As I let those words flow out of my mouth, I realize, I didn't book the Lyft. Gabe did, which means he knows where I stay. This isn't just a coincidence, and I can no longer justify it as a case of mistaken identity. Now I'm more scared than I've ever been in my life. I have too many questions, starting with who the fuck is Ryan?

Chapter 1

"Good morning, sunshine. Another long night?" Shelly says with a grin.

"Good morning Shelly. You know I rarely leave my house. I had a very peaceful night in, as usual." I flash the fakest smile.

"Oh, lighten up, Koni. A little birdie told me they saw you getting your party on. I should've known it was a lie. You're such a homebody."

"There is nothing like home, Shelly. You should try it. Can you email me a list of appointments for today when you get a chance?" rolling my eyes as I walk away. I'm panicking, although I'm doing an excellent job of not letting her see me sweat. I can't help but think about the chance someone really did see me last night. Knowing her, she'd be the first to know. I didn't see her in the crowd at the bar, or I wouldn't have even come into work today. Besides, it really isn't her place to comment on so everything is business as usual.

WALKING CONTRADICTION

I hate walking in this place damn near every day. I hate these people, and I hate the hour and 15-minute commute to get here every morning. The only thing worth discussing about *Given Investments* is the six-figure salary and the lifestyle it affords me. Our office is male dominated, like most corporate jobs. The only other woman, Nicole, always makes it her business to target me as her competition. If I bring in five new clients for the month, she aims for six. I think it's cute. I always take it as flattery, mostly because she never hits her goal.

I've never understood why she acts like I've done something to her. She is a cute middle eastern woman who always has extravagant eye makeup. Her lashes are generally large, but she works them. I think she's gorgeous and it's nice to have another woman in the office. She's relatively new and probably sees me as her main competition. I should just let her drive herself crazy while I continue to outrank her, but I rather give her tips to help her out.

The men are so caught up in each other; they hardly acknowledge us. Luckily, I don't have to interact with any of them consistently throughout the day. I only run into them when I first get into the office, at lunch, if they have a question about one of my clients or when it's time to leave. I don't have to be around anyone to need a push. I consider myself as my own competition, consistently placing at the top of our company amongst my other peers. I will be so happy when my other business ventures take off as I want. I really don't know what I was thinking, putting so much into this career field just for a check. I have no passion for this shit, and it has gotten old very quickly. And at 31, I am nowhere near retirement age. This worker bee shit is truly for the birds.

I walk into my office and close the door. I can smell my

favorite banana nut coffee greet me as I get closer to my desk. Shelly makes my coffee exactly right, every time. After the night I had, I was looking extra forward to it today. I must be losing my mind. Last night, in a place I swear I've never been, I woke up in a room full of people who would say otherwise. Down to a man that swore I was his long-term girlfriend—a fine ass man, but a man that isn't mine.

I planned on going back to get my car this morning, but it was outside waiting for me when I woke up. Which only served as a reassurance that it wasn't a horrible nightmare after all. I haven't stopped thinking about it since I got in that cab to go back to my apartment after dodging that creep. My life has been extremely healthy since being in Washington with Xay. I want a nice boring life for a while.

I'm so in my head this morning that I didn't notice there is a bouquet of beautiful sunflowers on my desk. My favorite! I already know who they're from; He always knows when I'm having one of those days. I walk over and set my purse on my desk as I pick up the card attached to the flowers. "Good morning baby, I know you wish you were anywhere but there, but it won't be long now. You are the best, and I'm so blessed to have such a beautiful soul like you in my life. And it doesn't hurt that you have a fat ass either. I love you. -Xay". I smile the biggest smile. He could sense that I wasn't in the best mood when I spoke to him on my way to work this morning, brushing it off when he asked as just a restless night and being sick of having to clock in for another person.

I haven't gotten around to tell him about last night yet. I don't even know if I want to. I still don't know how I got there; I just know that's where I woke up - on the floor at that, so I must have passed out. I may have been drunk, but

I don't drink like that anymore, nor do I go clubbing. Honestly, I rarely go anywhere. As Shelly said, I stay to myself and in the house.

My parents passed away when I was younger. My dad was murdered when I was 19, and my mom passed naturally of Lupus when I was 21. Losing them both in what felt like months apart opposed to years, messed me up pretty bad. That's around the time when I first began drinking heavily. It was hard adjusting without them both, my mom especially. My parents divorced when I was young, but she afforded me a nice middle-class upbringing with little support from my father.

His murder only affected me on an emotional level because I had so many 'what ifs' going on in my head. I thought he'd be able to walk me down the aisle, meet his grandchildren—if I ever have children and a plethora of other things that left me feeling empty. I knew I'd never be able to mend that relationship now, which caused me to lean on my mother even more for support. She didn't tell me she was sick until the last few months before her passing. She was always the epitome of strength and resilience; learning to cope without her has still been the hardest task of my life. She showed me my first sign of what it meant to be a woman and a boss, and that gave me the will to push through.

I have no siblings and the little family I do have, and my best friend, Tia, still lives in Arkansas. I honestly regret not staying home after completing Undergrad sometimes but moving to Washington was the best move for me to get my master's and advance quickly in my career. Xay and I luckily got into the same school for our master's and took it as a sign to move. I have a few associates here in Washington but no one solid enough to call a friend. Xay is the only other person that could get me out of the house, and he wasn't out last night, he doesn't go out much either.

I don't like club scenes, and I'm not big on being too social outside of work. My anxiety always ends up getting the best of me. I'd feel strange trying to explain something to Xay that I'm having a hard time explaining to myself. There's no way I can tell him without sounding bat shit crazy, drunk or high as hell. I pull my phone out of my purse and begin to text him something nasty to show my appreciation, but the second I pull my phone out, here comes nosey ass Shelly.

"Oohhh Koni, that man loves the hell out of you. You gotta teach me some of your tricks boss.", she sits a printout of appointments on my desk; something she could've easily emailed me.

She is by far the nosiest assistant I've ever had. I must give credit where it's due, though; she is extremely thorough, always does her job well, and most importantly, on time. That is way more than I can say about all the previous ones. She constantly asks me for tips on how to keep a man so in love. I honestly never know what to tell her, so I always just laugh it off.

"Start with a man that wants to be kept, because honey I've had my fair share of toads too."

She isn't a bad looking woman at all. She's always wearing this long blonde sew-in which suits her well. Her nails are always extra-long; it amazes me how she never skips a beat every time she has to type anything for me. Her medium brown skin is beautiful and blemish-free. She has a broad nose, full sexy lips and big eyes. She's always wearing different color contacts, so I don't know their actual color.

Her favorite contact color is grey which also suits her well.

She puts a lot into keeping her body fit and is always wearing something that compliments her shape. Her makeup is slayed every day. I don't think I've ever seen her without a full-face beat. Most times, she can be a little ghetto for my taste, but plenty of men stay checking for her. Hell, women too, when that's her thing.

She dates all types from what she tells me, so I'm not sure why nothing has stuck for her yet relationship-wise. It could have a big part to do with the fact that she never stays in her own business long enough. I watch as she picks up one of my flowers, holds it to her nose and inhales deeply as she usually does whenever I get them. She looks at me and waves her hand in brushing off manner.

"Yea, yea, boss lady. You just want to keep all the secrets to yaself." she says, followed by a giggle as she walks out and closes the door. It's a constant reminder not to take what Xay gives me for granted. He always knows just what to say and when to say it. He is truly God's gift.

I pick up my phone and finish my text. "You are the best baby. You always know just what to say. Can't wait to see you later and sit this fat ass on your dick. Can you tell? I love you!" *Send*. I proceed to put my hand under my pink pleated skirt and slide my panties to the side; I dip my finger in just enough to show him this drip, take a picture and send it to go with the text. I love that he goes out of his way to make sure that I am ok in every sense. I'll be damned if I ever let an opportunity to show him pass me by. I still get butterflies every time I'm with him.

Xavier made every other time I thought I was in love seem like child's play. That puppy love people talk about; I didn't know how real it was until I met him. My past lovers could never compare. Women love his 6'3, slim, chocolate frame. I mean, they absolutely cannot get enough.

I always watch women as they check him out whenever we do decide to go out on the town. They stay trying to come on to him when I am out of his reach; some will even try to steal feels. I guess they try to check to see if the dick fits the rest of the package. It does. He always tells them he's taken and points over at me as he adds his disclaimer that 'unless my girl is interested in having you.' They usually glance my way and roll their eyes as they walk away. Some are with it and begin to walk towards me to see if they can join. Every time it happens, it makes me feel good that he's wanted by so many and still chooses me every time.

I remember when we first met back in college. I had just gone through a messy breakup, and the last thing I was thinking about was another headache or heartbreak. The only reason I was out that night was that my girls decided they had had enough of my seclusion. They wanted to help me get out of my funk, so they forced me to go to dinner. They had been telling me for weeks about a group of guys they had met and thought I would like their company because they were genuinely a good funny group. To my surprise, they were the coolest group of men I had met in a while.

I was twirling my hair as a nervous habit when Xavier asked, "Are you horny? Because you just a keep pulling that hair". I laughed so hard, thinking that was bold of him. Who asks a stranger such a weird question? But I needed that laugh. Xavier Butler, I will never forget that day. My girls and his guys became the best of friends in college. We ate lunch together, ate dinner, went to college parties and even had movie nights. We were together so much; people always would think we were on group couples' outings.

One night, we had a movie night in one of my homegirls' dorm room. That's when it bloomed into a little more. He stole my number. No bullshit, stole my number. It was funny at the time because I had my phone set up to where if I called a number, not in my contacts, it would show on their end as unknown. He called himself being slick and asked for my phone to get someone's number. I didn't think twice and gave it to him. He called himself without me knowing.

"Do you have your phone number blocked or something?"

"What? Blocked? What do you mean?"

"Because it's showing up as unknown."

"Huh? I didn't call you."

"I know. Is it blocked? How are you even able to do that?"

I started laughing because I had finally realized he was trying to get my number without asking. So, I threw a hint about texting from it instead. That was the beginning of something beautiful. Although neither of us was truly ready for a relationship in college, that didn't stop us from messing around when time permitted. We went through a lot, being young, dumb and indecisive. But the majority of the nonsense came from me being unwilling to give in to my true feelings for him. From the beginning, he showed me the lengths he would go for me. Fast forward to nine years later, and we are still kicking. I will never let this one go.

Getting sidetracked with my thoughts of him is serving as a distraction from last night's mess. I snap out of my daydream of all the freaky things I'm going to do to Xay when I get off when Shelly buzzes in to ask if I had forgotten about my first meeting today. I glance over at my clock, and its 9:33 a.m. already. Fuck. I'm three minutes late, what a bad impression on a new client, especially for me being a financial advisor. Tardiness looks irresponsible. I hurry and gather the paperwork this new client sent prior to our meeting today and rush to the front to greet him.

I nearly drop the folder when I look at this man. He is stunning, the sexiest older man I've ever seen in my life. He is a redbone with a tall, broad, thick build. His beautiful neat long salt and pepper locs are styled to the back and compliment his full gray thick beard. He either has a stylist or his taste in clothing is impeccable. He is dressed in a perfectly tailored all black suit with a gray tie to accent the specs of gray in his dress shoes. I know I've been standing here for a full minute, just staring in silence. He breaks it by extending his hand.

"Hello, I am Gabriel Grove. You must be Koni Reese?" he says as he smiles, showing off a set of beautiful pearly white teeth. His voice is deep and sultry. His name makes me think of last night, and how he even looks similar to the Gabe from the bar but even better. All these fine ass men just falling from the sky lately. And as if he could get any finer, his dimple flashes as he waits for a response from me. I take his hand and shake.

"Yes, I'm Koni. It's nice to meet you, Gabriel. I apologize for my tardiness, let's go into my office so we can get started. Follow me." I turn and walk towards my office. Shelly intentionally knocks some papers off her desk and gets up dramatically to retrieve them. She stops and puts her ass right in his view as she bends over in her short dress to pick up her mess. I can see him peep at what she was trying to show as we continue into my office and close the door. That girl can be so damn extra at times.

"Please, have a seat. Tell me a little about why you think a financial advisor is necessary for you at this point in your career? I see you mostly invest in other businesses, correct?" I say as I pull out my chair and have a seat.

"Well, Koni, I feel that at this point, my investments need protecting. If I can be honest with you, I'm a street nigga at heart but a businessman first. I used to do less than desirable things to get my money, and now I have my money work for me. I want my children to continue to be set without ever having to live the life I had to. I want to be completely legal and need someone with the skill set to make sure that I continue to make wise investments and help pave my future further. I have invested and helped others start over 20 businesses. I currently own one local business of my own, a bar, down on 22nd street. It's my baby, but I travel so much trying to keep up with the other investments that I hardly have the time to stop by. My son runs it for me. I came to you because a friend of his recommended you as the best in town. I trust that you will help me get to where I want to be." He flashes that dimple again.

I've worked with many men who, as they like to say, 'got it out of the mud.' - Basically robbing, killing and dealing until they stacked enough money to escape that world. I've never been one to judge someone that wants and sets out to do better for themselves. Looking at him today, I wouldn't have guessed he came from a hood background. He presented his cover well, so no-one would ever be able to judge him that way. As we begin to speak more candidly,

I can hear a bit of his hood accent. He remains very professional and cloaks it well.

He tells me how he did a twelve-year sentence in prison on some drug-related charges and how he no longer wishes to live that lifestyle. He goes into how being away that long took his opportunity to be close to his children and how it is his biggest regret in life. He uses them as motivation and is currently focusing a lot of his energy into mending those broken relationships in his life and making sure they have as least worries as possible. We discuss a few plans on how to get his money to work smarter in the long run. We go over the investments that are ultimately losing and plan to either make them profitable or drop them. The meeting lasts close to two hours. He seems like an already financially literate man, and I'm glad he chose me as his advisor.

"Mrs. Reese, it was nice meeting you. I think this partnership will be greatly beneficial to us both. I brought something to show my appreciation for you taking me on as a client. I can tell you are going to take me right where I am trying to get. I will see you soon," he says as he hands me a black envelope sealed with a gold initialed sticker.

"You didn't have to get me anything. It is enough that you chose me to handle such an important task. You will not regret it. See you soon Mr. Grove." I watch him as he finds his way out.

He's already rich; I plan to make him wealthy. He may just be my biggest client yet. I open the envelope to see what is in it because even with me telling him he shouldn't have; I love getting gifts from my clients. It's a thank you card, and inside the card, he has inserted a check for $10,000. The memo line reads, "I hope you're ready." My mouth falls open as the envelope begins to slip from my hand. I'm shocked.

I deal with many wealthy people, but my regular fee is steep on its own. I've gotten a few bonuses from past clients, but nothing this substantial after only one consultation meeting. I can tell he's serious about wanting to be completely legit, and I am ready for anything that comes my way. Immediately after he leaves, Shelly makes her way into my office to get any information she can get on him.

"Well, I know he has money if he is in here talking to you. Because I don't know anybody that can even afford your services. That man was too damn fine. And those sexy ass dreads, girl, I could've just melted in his lap if he let me. Did he mention anything about a wife? Girlfriend? I didn't see a ring, but I need to know. Hell, who am I kidding, I wouldn't care if he was the way he looks." She bites down on her lip in a seductive way and begins to laugh.

"Shelly, this was our first meeting as you know. I need you to keep yourself tamed until I become more comfortable with him as a client. I don't need any extra mess. I have a good feeling that he is the client I need to finish my personal goals. So please, just behave."

"Behave? Koni, you not the only one that knows how to act all high class around here, ma'am. He must got money? I'll leave him alone, but I can't promise you that I won't bite back if he bites." She flips her hair and walks back out to her desk.

I really don't need anything messing this up for me. Shit, ten thousand dollars. He will be the reason that I am finally able to start my boutique and edibles food truck. I am claiming it. The rest of the workday seems to go by quickly. I've managed to keep last night out of my thoughts since getting that extra boost in my day. He's my only new client for this week, so everyone else is just 15 minutes here and there to update their earning profiles.

My job isn't really that bad honestly. I just hate the idea of working so hard for anyone while having to neglect my dreams. It's finally time to go home. I speed out of the parking lot, as usual, trying to beat the halt of rush hour traffic. Having that encounter with that fine ass man just made me want to get back to my man even more. We have plans to meet up later for dinner. I planned to cook a nice meal and stay in like we usually opt to do, but now I feel like celebrating, so I call him up.

"Baby, you feel like celebrating tonight?"

"Hey, sexy! Celebrating what?"

"I got a new client today. He even gave me a sign-on bonus for accepting him as a client. I think this may be the break I've been looking for, and I just feel so good I want to go out and celebrate —on me, of course, so what do you say?" Already knowing he would agree.

"Look at you baby, Congratulations. That's great news; it sounds like your bad day got turned around after all. And of course, we gotta celebrate this win for my baby. I'm so proud of you."

"Ok, great! We can go to Ocean's Steakhouse tonight! They have the best sushi. So, I will see you around 7, right?"

"I'll be there at 6, I been waiting to taste that drip you sent me earlier all day. I want my dessert before dinner. I love you. See yo fine ass soon.", he says and hangs up the phone.

It sends chills down my spine. Well, it sends throbs to my pussy, to be more accurate. I blast my "Fuck Me Harder" playlist on Apple Music all the way home to set my mood more. Once I finally get home, I see Xay hasn't made it yet, which is perfect because I always like to do a little freshen up after being at work all day. I get out of the car, check the mail and go inside my condo. Eucalyptus and spearmint greet me as I walk into the door. This scent is one from the Bath and Body Works aromatherapy selection that helps to reduce stress. A lot of people don't believe a scent can help, but when I walk into my door, it's like a huge weight is being lifted from my shoulders every day, it works for me.

I get naked before I can even close the door all the way. I hop in the shower and take a quick one because I know I will more than likely just go right back in after Xay comes and shows out. I put the pleated skirt back on for esthetics and hear him pull into the driveway. Right on time. I lay back on my black suede couch, with my legs spread wide open. I get in position so that when he walks in, I'm all that he sees. I hear his key turn the lock and watch him as he walks in the door. He gives me the sexiest smile and drops everything as he closes the door.

"Just like I like. Look at you being a good girl," he says almost in my reach.

He comes over and kisses me on the lips and then travels to kiss my other lips. He makes a comment about the drip being just as good as it looked in the picture. I blush a little; he still has that effect on me. He picks me up and carries me over to the doorway entry half table and sits me on it against the wall. With my legs now dangling off the table, he lifts my skirt and buries his head in my pussy. I moan so loud and grab the back of his neck.

He's licking on my clit when he takes one hand and puts two fingers in my pussy. He starts the tickling motion, the one that always hits my g-spot and drives me wild. He's sucking on my clit while going back and forth with his fingers. I start to scream as I pull his neck harder and wrap my legs around his head. He won't stop. I feel myself lose control and my body starts to convulse. I'm cumming, but he won't let me go. I'm squirming, and he won't let me free.

"Baby, please, I can't take it. I can't take this. This shit too good." I yell. My moans get even louder as he starts to mumble how good my cum tastes with my pussy still in his mouth. He starts moaning too, and that shit takes me over the edge. I begin to cum again all over his face; he still won't let me go. I push back so hard he has no choice but to back away. I hop off the table and get on my knees. I can feel myself still cumming.

"Put your dick in my mouth now," I command, looking up at him and sticking my tongue out.

He pulls it out, and of course, it's already rock hard and ready. I sit there on my knees and begin to swirl my tongue around the tip. He's still moaning. I lick his balls and come back up and move my tongue down the length of his dick until I get to the tip. I begin to swirl my tongue around it. I'm looking in his eyes as I move up and down. I place one hand on his lower back for more leverage and use the other hand to fondle his balls lightly. I know he loves it when I do this.

"Cum for me, baby. Shoot it wherever you'd like." I moan with his dick still in my mouth. I can feel his body tense up, his eyes close and his head falls back. He pulls back and shoots it all over my titties. I try my hardest to catch some in my mouth, and of course, I'm successful. He always tastes so good to me. He picks me up and carries me to the bathroom. He starts the water and tells me to get in. I get in, and he follows. He pushes me against the wall and starts to pound my pussy from the back. I feel the water as it runs through my curls and bounces off of our bodies. We fuck for a good twelve minutes until we both cum again. We shower and begin getting dressed for dinner.

"Koni, you got the best pussy I've ever had. And I'm not just saying that because I'm with you. You do something to me that I can't explain. You are my soulmate. Sexually, mentally and spiritually. You are all I need, baby." He says as he leaves me in the bathroom to do my hair and makeup.

"Xay, you know I feel the same. I prayed for you, and God showed the fuck out."

I can hear him in my bedroom shuffling through the closet. We both have sections of each other's closets with our belonging, as well as drawer space. We spend a lot of time with each other, typically, about four nights a week. It's usually the full weekend and one weekday. Our work schedules are over-demanding, so we try not to distract each other too much during the week.

He is an engineer and works his ass off. He also wants to open his own business that will allow him to relax a little more than what he is able to right now. Like me, he also chose his career for a check. He isn't passionate about it, but it affords him a nice lifestyle as well. He's constantly showering me with expensive gifts. I'm not much of a material person, but I love that he gives me such beautiful things.

My second bedroom looks like a closet of the rich, famous and freaky. I put all the clothes, shoes, jewelry and expensive artwork in that room. It showcases a different style than my own. Where my home is minimalistic, that room is full of beautiful worldly possessions, even down to the brand-new clothing that I've never worn. I only go in there on special occasions. For me, it is a room that showcases love and a glimpse of who I sometimes wish I could openly be. My anxiety is so extreme; it's almost crippling.

Everything in my home is neutral except that room. Black has always been my favorite color, which is extremely obvious in my decorating style. But the walls in that room are painted white, with specs of real gold splattered over the walls. Xay said I threw a tantrum one day until I got them. Although that sounds nothing like me, I'll let him roll with whatever floats his boat. All he had to say is he really wanted the walls. They are incredibly beautiful.

The rug is real fur that he had shipped in from Italy. I mentioned to him that I value things from other countries, so he has filled that room with just that. And the freaky part? We buy a new sex toy every month we are together, as our own celebration. This is our fourth year together officially as a couple, and we have something for every single month. And to keep them out of view and reach, I store them in that room. I never have overnight guests, so no one else ever goes in there.

Our sex life is fantastic; we rarely use the things we buy. We pretty much have a collection of things that we may try one day, I guess if we get bored enough. We have swings, toys, cuffs, plugs, honestly almost anything you could imagine. I'm perfectly fine with our sex without any additional help, but it's always fun to go pick out something new to add. I hardly go in there, but when I do, I always see something new that he must've added when I wasn't looking. New lingerie or heels, things that I wouldn't usually pick for myself, but they always look damn good when I do decide to wear them.

I know he spends his extra time in there because sometimes he leaves food and liquor behind. I never mind or ask him about it; I just clean it up when I notice. He gives me no reason to complain. He truly spoils me in every single way. He appreciates everything about me, and we don't even argue. I have never had anything like this.

I walk into my bedroom, and he is already dressed, sitting on the edge of the bed just looking at me. Even the way his eyes gleam every time he sees me, I don't know what I did to deserve this man, but if it's up to me, I will never do anything to lose him. That includes figuring out what the hell is wrong with me before it spills over into my real life. This isn't the first time this black-out thing has happened to me since my drunk college days. I pretty much drowned inside a bottle of Jack Daniels as much as I could during that time. I have had a couple of occasions that I couldn't remember how I got here or there or sometimes something as simple as when I got dressed.

I've always brushed it off as a memory issue or blamed it on the alcohol until last night. It's never been this severe. I used to see a therapist for what she diagnosed as PTSD when I was in college. I thought you could only get that from going to war, so I was confused by the diagnosis. My psychiatrist at the time said that it was due to something that I may have omitted from childhood, but in her 'well-trained opinion' it stemmed from a toxic relationship I had, while in college. After she explained it a little more, it all made sense. I thought I was well past the years of having to pay someone to talk my problems out, but right now, I can't see any other step that would make sense. I need to get back to my full self again, so I will be setting up an appointment first thing tomorrow morning. Tonight though, is going to be one to go down in the books.

Chapter 2

Last night was all one big blur. Dinner was delicious; the drinks were even better. I think I celebrated a little too much. We decided to go out dancing after dinner, and that's honestly the last thing I remember. Which I'm a little thrown off by, considering what happened the night before, but last night was different.

I was with my favorite person, having the time of our lives. I begin to slide my hands around my black silk sheets, searching for Xay. I glance over at the clock sitting on my nightstand and see it's 6:23 am, more than likely he has already headed out for work. He goes in an hour before me every day. My body feels amazing like I just finished having the best sex of my life. I'm in the mood for another round, but since Xay isn't here, I'll just take care of it myself. I reach for the nightstand and pull the top drawer open; my rabbit isn't in here.

It's not like I use it anywhere else, so I'm unsure of where it could be. I have another one that we haven't opened in the guest room. I guess today is the day to crack that baby open. I slide out of bed and step down onto my black faux fur rug that sits under my bed and feel something cold under my foot. I reach over and flick my lamp on. When I look down, I see an anal plug that we bought sometime last year but never used. It's designed to look like a furry pink tail when inserted. Xay picked this one out.

I begin to look around the room. It's a mess. It looks like we broke out a few new toys last night and left all the packaging on the floor. I can't remember any of the new toys, but by the open ones, we had an even better night than I thought. I begin to pick up the packages and straighten the room as I go. Before I know it, it's time to start getting ready for work.

I still haven't found my rabbit and don't have time to look for the unused one. That means no orgasm for me this morning. I take a quick shower, throw my hair in a sleek low bun, and throw on a mid-length skin-tight yellow dress with an oversized tribal vest. I group it with my favorite orange chunky pumps. I head towards the kitchen to begin to make my morning smoothie. As I am reaching for the refrigerator handle, I see that Xay left a note on my dry erase board. It reads, 'You showed the fuck out last night, you deserve to sleep in. I like the role play, don't let it be the last time.'

He leaves me sweet notes on it all the time. This one, I wish I could remember because the way my bedroom looks, I bet it was something like a movie. I don't know what the hell he is talking about with the role play, that's something that we hadn't gotten around to trying yet, but apparently, we tried it last night. I wonder who we were. I don't care too much; I'm satisfied to know that he had a great night. We both hadn't stepped foot in a club in a minute, so it was much needed, and from what I did remember, the most fun we've had out in a while. I grab my ingredients, finish making my smoothie, and make my way to work.

This morning, not even Shelly can ruin this great mood I am in. I get to the office, and Shelly has a printout of appointments on my desk sitting next to my coffee. She hasn't come back here to bother me yet. I do like how our offices are set up with privacy in mind. Our building is huge, 13 stories, to be exact. We have a total of twenty advisors, and each one of us has our side of the floor.

When the elevators open on each floor, there is a beautifully decorated lobby area for the assistants and clients to lounge. Directly behind each assistant's desk, there is a large office for each advisor. The offices are private and fully closed in. Clients often comment on how nice the setup is. I still admire it daily. Once I finish my coffee, I call my old therapist, Dr. Rainey.

"Hey Koni, it's been a while. Are you ok?" she sounds a little concerned.

"I'm fine. Or no. I'm not ok, but I felt fine until this week. I think I should come in for a visit. Do you have any upcoming appointments available? I need the soonest you have."

"That doesn't sound good. Are you having suicidal thoughts? What's going on?", she questions.

"No, none of that. I just really feel I'd benefit from talking to you right now. What's your next available appointment?" I lie a little to calm her down.

"Oh, ok. Well, my next available slot isn't until Tuesday

at noon. Will that work for you?"

"I'm going to make it work. See you Tuesday!"

"Ok, if you need me before then, just give me a call. See you soon." She hangs up. I know she's worried. I didn't tell her too much, because knowing her, she'd probably just try to have me hospitalized. Hell, at this point if I were her, I'd probably hospitalize me too.

It's a dull day as far as the workload goes. I'm looking through my client's profiles when my phone chimes for a text message. I check the message; it's from Tia. 'Hey! Just got in town for a business trip, kinda. Lol, free to do lunch today?' Perfect timing. I respond immediately, 'Girl, you are right on time! Lunch sounds great. Anywhere in mind?' I decide to take a half-day and enjoy some girl time with my best friend. Tia and I have been friends since high school. An old mutual friend introduced us one day, and we've been tight ever since. Tia always comes with the tea and never sugar-coats a thing. She has saved my ass so many times. She knows all my dirt and vice versa. She's the only person that I communicate with, in my personal life regularly, aside from Xay.

She is here to meet with one of her clients from her self-started business. She runs a steady-growing social media P.R. firm. Watching her full growth throughout this business journey has been nothing short of motivational. I've always wanted to own my own and be self-sufficient, but watching her reminded me to have the drive, and to keep going through it all. I'm a product of hard work, but the drive was something that I struggled with until recently. Between her and Xay, I can't thank them enough just for genuinely being themselves, and allowing me to be mine, no matter what.

I am so happy to be finally getting to catch up with Tia. I haven't caught her up on any of the things that have gone down in the last couple of days. I didn't want her to worry about me with her being so far away. Today, however, I have to tell her. I think it's better in a face-to-face setting, that way she'll be able to see that I am in a sane mind as I speak. It's been about seven months since I last saw her face-to-face, so this girl time is much needed.

She texts me an address, I put it in my G.P.S. and head towards the restaurant. It's a place she saw on Yelp with great reviews. I've never had it myself, so I'm all for trying a new place. I arrive at the restaurant and see it looks crowded. The building is unique; it has a large wooden frame shaped like a chest with the name 'Juicy Treasures,' painted on it in gold. It's a crab boil style restaurant and has a very relaxed feel to it. It's cool for me because seafood is my favorite. Watching a few people walk in, I already wish I were a bit more casual. I see Tia getting out of her car at the same time as I'm getting out of mine.

"Tiaaaa! Damn baddie, where you going?" I asked, hyping her like I usually do.

She looks up. She's dressed in black biker shorts, a crop baby pink hoodie and the cutest pair of olive strappy stilettos. One thing about her was she was always going to dress her ass off. Her light skin is glowing, and her petite body in perfect shape. She looks beautiful.

"Koniiii, it's been forever! Girl come here!" she shouts as she begins to run towards me. We hug and do our typical bullshitting and cracking jokes about how long it's been as we walk in and get seated. Our waitress is sweet and not over-bearing, which is perfect because it still gives me a private enough vibe to be able to have an open conversation.

"So, you know the client I came to see, right?"

"The same one you've had for a couple of years from here, right? Or you got another one?"

"No, the same one. Well, we are finally dating publicly, and I want you to meet him while I'm down here. And before you start your shit, I told you when we started talking. But we both wanted privacy to see if it was something worth talking about. And honey, he is so damn amazing. He's a good one, like Xay. It's been about five months. I know y'all will like each other."

"Oh, so that means I'll be seeing you a little more often then! I know you're going to be flying down here to see your boo all the time now. Look at you keeping secrets and getting in whole relationships and shit. Congrats, girl."

"First of all, I'm going to be getting 'flewed out.' Period! Girl, Darius wouldn't let me buy a ticket even if I wanted to. And I hate you so much. I knew you were gone come with that shit."

We both start laughing. I'm so happy for her. She deserves to be happy with a good man. She has told me many things about him as her client, and if I were paying enough attention, I would've noticed the increase of conversations she had been holding about him. I knew she was crushing from the first time she talked about him. Hell, we both were talking about how fine he was before we ever knew anything about him. Social media exposes you to strangers all day, and he is one we just happened to creep on often. I still remember the day he reached out to her about gaining her services. You'd have thought she hit the lottery, and in retrospect, she just may have.

He is fine as hell; real Zaddy-ish. He has an athletic build, brown-skinned, usually wears a low fade with a sexy thick beard. He's smart, someone surprisingly from our hometown, just someone we didn't grow up with. He built his way up by starting a moving app. The app took off, and he became an instant millionaire. Tia has stressed so many times how her next man will not be a broke one. Putting that energy in the air has finally paid off for her. Tia was always set to be some rich person's trophy wife, and now she may be on the verge of living out her full life's dream.

"All jokes aside, I am so proud of you! You are living our dream, and baby, I'm not too far off. Remember those years when I had to convince you we'd make it? Look at our fancy asses now. We worked and will continue to work for everything we want. We are real boss bitch goals."

"Ayeee. To us then, Koni!"

"To us!" We tap our glasses and I down my glass of Pinot Noir. Tia does the same and signals towards our waitress for a second round.

"Well, my life is pretty basic. You know, because I keep you updated on my life when we have those weekly phone conversations,' I say, throwing all the shade her way with a smirk on my face. 'Even though I pretty much did the same thing by not telling you this sooner.' I wave my hand as I see her lips forming words to interrupt me. 'Xay and I are as good as we could be, so no, it's not that. But I do have news. I had another blackout, possibly more than one. I woke up in an unfamiliar place. And before you start, no, I was not drunk. You know I laid off the excess drinking years ago, this time something's different."

"What do you mean blackouts? If you weren't drunk? Like just waking up in random places and shit?"

"Yes, exactly that. A couple of nights ago, I woke up around 2 a.m. in a foreign bar with foreign people who I had never met, but a few seemed very fond of me. I even met a man that acted as if we're dating, but I swear I've never seen him before that night."

"Girl, what? I hope you're ok. You don't remember how you got there? Hell, that sounds worse than college. You used to blackout, but I could barely tell a difference in you. And the scariest thing you probably could've gotten into was a whole lot of fucking,' she laughs. "Was your other man fine?" She continues to laugh.

"I know you're trying to be funny whore, but yes girl! He was so damn fine. The man looked like a damn God. Hell, I thought I was dreaming just because he looks like a dreamy ass nigga if I ever saw one." We both burst into laughter.

This was the first time I laughed about the situation since it's happened. I immediately begin filling her in with the details from that night and last night, or at least what I could remember. I really should've told her when it first happened. She always knows what to say. I'm just not in a place to even try to process what is going on. Talking to her makes me feel not as crazy, even with her calling me crazy a hundred times while talking about it.

She agrees with going back to the psychiatrist. She also suggests it could just be my hormones because I'm naturally moody. Which is a good point, but I know this is different.

We both agree it wouldn't explain the blackout. Even with all my crazy mood changes, I've never woken up with strangers. We continue to enjoy our lunch and finish catching up on what's been going on with work, our families and our men. We agree to meet again before she leaves. We hug and part ways.

The time flew by so quickly. We sat there for over 3 hours, just talking, eating and day drinking. And now that I have the rest of my day free and a nice little buzz, I'm going to take myself shopping. I can get into the idea of role-playing, and I've been thinking about it all day. I really want to do a few scenarios but think that I may get awkward during sex if I'm trying to pretend to be someone else. I am generally awkward during sex anyway. Although with Xay, I have gotten to a certain level of comfort.

He makes me feel like I can do no wrong, like no one can out sexy me, which makes me brave and more confident than I usually am, sexually. With him, I can be me without censorship. I don't have the additional worry of whether he's judging me for being too nasty or too quiet. I don't obsess as much on the areas I may not measure up, as I would with a stranger or new mate. He has never made me question myself. Even with all that, I still have shy days with him. Some nights I may get so in my head about trying something new that I let it psych me out.

So, him saying we tried role play, is a little of a shock. However, I'm fully ready to explore all the new personas I can be. I already know what my principal, prostitute, stripper and random chick at a bar name will be. Just as I am picking up the cutest navy and pink polka dot blouse to compliment a sexy white skirt suit to complete my principal giddup, my phone begins to ring. It's Xay. Right on time.

"Hey baby! How'd lunch go?"

"It was great! It was so good getting to see Tia and having a little girl time to really catch up. I'm out shopping now since I'm off for the rest of the day. I was just thinking about you. We had fun last night huh?" I ask in hopes of getting him to give me more details on the role play.

"Hell yea. I've been thinking about you and Ryan all day. When you try something new, your ass goes big. Now I have two girlfriends," he laughs.

I feel like my ears are playing tricks on me. Ryan? Again with this damn name. But he said we role-played. I was pretty drunk and can't remember, so it's possible I used the name from the bar when role-playing. Xay has never mentioned the name before today. This is completely blowing my mood. What the fuck does he mean he has two girlfriends now? I was so out of it; I could've invited someone from the club into our bed. That would make a lot of sense with the way my bedroom looked this morning. Fuck.

"Baby?" I hear him chime in to break my overflowing thoughts.

"Yea, I'm here. Sorry I was a little distracted, trying to find these shoes." I try to sound unfazed.

"Well, I'll let you get back to your shopping. I just wanted to check on you. And to make sure she doesn't stay hidden from me for too long, I miss her already.' He laughs, "And you too baby. I love you."

"I don't think I could hide her; even if I tried," I forced a laugh. "I love you too, baby. Talk to you later."

I hold the phone until I hear him hang up. My mind is in overdrive with questions that I should be asking him, but I decide to wait until after meeting up with Dr. Rainey to mention it. I want to avoid all things that may alter him being in my future. Even though he seemingly likes this change, I can't say the same. Blacking out and acting like someone else? The thought is scarier than I can process. I'm looking forward to getting some solid answers.

Chapter 3

"He called you the same name that those creeps were calling you? Damn, I don't think I've ever heard you use the fake name Ryan, so I'm not sure about that. Remember Quinn from high school? I think that was my favorite nickname for you, that or KitKat." Tia and I both start laughing, reminiscing over all the horrible nicknames from back then. All I can see is her long curly hair flipping back and forth on my iPhone screen.

"Girl. I don't know where that would come from either. The only reason Ryan registers with me is because I've considered it as a child's name when the time comes for me to have a little rugrat. Specifically, a girl, because I always thought that it was one of those cute unisex names that sound better on girls."

"I kinda remember you mentioning that too. But that still doesn't make sense. He said two girlfriends, so maybe you did bring someone else in? You said it was a mess, and y'all used shit you've never used before. Hell, you like women, I can easily see that."

"I know, but that wouldn't explain the whole bar thing.

Xay and I have had threesomes before. He said something about role play, and I don't want to ask too much because then he will know something is off."

"I don't know why you're trying to keep this from him. That man loves your dirty draws. We haven't been able to get him to shut up about your ass since college. I think if he loved you then, he would definitely love your weird-ass enough to be able to handle this now."

She's right. I know that Xay would be open to being here for me throughout the full process, good or bad. The thing that was throwing me off was the whole bar scene. None of it made sense to me. Since Xay mentioned Ryan, I now am led to believe that some of the things Rocky and Gabe said were true. And if any portion is true, I feel like I should fully get rid of those problems before involving Xay in trying to fix myself yet again.

"I know he does and would. I just think I should find out the whole ordeal with Mr. Dreamy and Rocky, don't you think?"

"Good point. Maybe you can go back to the bar? Oh, I know! We can go together just in case any shit pops off. Plus, that gives us a chance to get out and party a little together."

"That's a good idea. When do you leave out? Tomorrow?"

"No, I'll be here for another four days. Darius cancelled my original flight home after telling him I was free the whole week. So, I'll have more time with you. But we can go tonight? It's Friday; I'd bet at least one of them will be in there."

"Cool. Xay isn't coming over tonight, so I am completely free. Sounds like a plan. Maybe around 11:00 tonight?"

"11 works for me. I'll be at your place around ten o'clock to pregame. Please have your ass ready because we both know how long it takes you." We both laugh, knowing how true it is. Hell, I might as well start getting ready now.

I hang up our FaceTime call and can hear someone out in the lobby talking to Shelly. It is more than likely my next client just a little early. Mrs. Boch is an older white woman that you can tell has had every surgery money can buy. She's holding up pretty nice to be in her late sixties. You can tell her work has always been well done. I decided to call her in early to go ahead and free the rest of her day up.

"Nice to see you again, Mrs. Boch. I see that you're prompt as always. Please come in and make yourself comfortable."

"Koni, so beautiful as always. What I wouldn't give to be 30 again."

"You can't tell that you're too far from it."

"You sure as hell better not be able to --with as much money as this all costs," she says, extending her hand and moving it down the length of her body.

She makes herself comfortable on my black leather love seat. We go over her profits as I advise her that her stores are coming in exceedingly high in loss. I tell her that it may be good to focus her energy more on making her online shop the chosen method. I try educating her that a lot of large stores are closing many, if not all, of their physical locations because online shopping is becoming more popular than the traditional method. She is old school, so she still wants to focus on driving customers to her shops. I tell her it's her choice, but it's truly her biggest loss right now.

"Well, no disregard for what you're saying. But I can afford to take a loss or two. I love building relationships with my clients, and many of those who supported me from the beginning still visit me. Sometimes, It's not all about the money."

I can understand that, but it's still my place to advise her on the best financial route. We continue until we come to a compromise to at least cover the loss expenses. We set our next appointment for two weeks from now, and I watch her sway her much younger body away. I'm thankful for my clients because they push me to think outside of the box. Hearing all their success stories that come with plenty of failures, is daily motivation. I want it all.

"Boss lady, your last appointment canceled for today. We're free for the rest of the day. Mind if I dip out early? I've got everything ready to go," Shelly asks through the intercom system. I was starting to think she didn't know how to use the damn thing, but now I see she only uses it when she wants to ask something without being in my face.

"Go ahead, Shelly. Thank you. Have a good weekend. See you Monday."

"Thanks! You too, Koni. Get out and live a little! See ya Monday boss."

I enjoy the days she asks to leave early when we're

down. She's so organized and never misses a beat. Her leaving never has a negative impact, so I don't mind. I don't even mind that she always claims her 40 hours no matter how early she leaves. I always use this time to reflect on where I am. Right now, my nerves are shot. I don't know what to expect by going back to this bar tonight, but I'm so glad that I don't have to go back there alone. I don't even know what I am going to say if I happen to see either of them. They already think I'm crazy. I decide to leave a little early myself to get home to mentally and physically prepare for the night.

I walk into my door and immediately notice I must be out of my oil. I don't feel the instant relief upon entry, a day where it would be most useful. I walk over to the kitchen and erase the dry erase board on the fridge. I start a to do list, with my oil at the top of the list. I feel antsy. I'm honestly surprised I haven't sent myself into another anxiety attack. Times like this I wish I still smoked enough to keep it in the house. An edible won't do what I need. Right now, I need instant relief.

I walk to the bathroom, where I made sure to make a mental note that my missing vibrator was there on the side of the shower earlier. I pick it off my rug and quickly rinse it. I shake the excess water off and grab a lighter with my free hand as I walk out of the bathroom towards my bedroom. I light a candle on my dresser, hop in my bed and turn my vibrator on its lowest setting.

"Alexa, play 'Self Cums First' playlist on shuffle."

"Ok, one moment," the automated smart home system responds. There is a slight pause before *Lullaby* by Umi (feat Yeek) blares through the speaker. This is a perfect song for the occasion. The light vibrations on my clit match the pace of the song. I feel the tension beginning to leave my body as my pussy slowly becomes more moist. I move my free hand up to pull both breasts out of my bra. I pull my shirt back down so that the fabric covers both nipples. I quickly flick my finger over each nipple through the fabric, alternating back and forth. The texture of the fabric adds a unique sensation. I reposition my hand on my vibrator to click the button at the base to quicken the speed and deepen the vibration. My sensitive clit reacts immediately to the intensity. Within seconds my legs begin to shake. I moan loudly as I fight through the urge to force the hand holding the vibrator away. I quickly lose the battle and pull the vibrator away to stop myself from cumming so soon.

Seeing that I hardly ever have free time to get in self sessions, quickies are the norm. But today, I have time; there is no need to rush. I continue to bring myself to the edge of climax and pulling away each time, right before I erupt. My body begins to shake uncontrollably, and I let out a high-pitched moan; occasionally bringing the vibrator from my clit up to alternate between nipples. As I begin to squirm around the bed, I notice my pussy leaving small wet spots on my sheets. Looking at the pre-cum stains sends me over the edge. I clench the vibrator between my thighs to keep it directly on my clit as I move my hands up to my breasts. I pinch each nipple as hard as I can stand. My body becomes tense as I involuntarily kick my legs in the air and spread them wide. The vibrator begins to slowly roll down my clit just as I begin to squirt uncontrollably. I feel my body begin to relax. I click the vibrator until it stops buzzing in my hand. I stretch my body out in the middle of the bed, fighting my heavy eyelids, as I quickly lose the battle.

"So, what is the plan if we see them? Do you have questions planned? We telling them off? Or what?" Tia asks as she passes me her T.H.C. vape pen. I hold the button and take a long draw. It's something flavored. Still some medicinal quality, but it tastes like Jolly Ranchers. They're doing so much with weed these days, it's amazing. I follow the hit by chugging down my third glass of wine.

"Hell if I know. I was trying to come up with a plan the entire time I was getting ready, and I still have nothing. So, I'm just going to wing it," I say, shrugging my shoulders.

"Wing it? Well, this should be good. It's 11:02 now, let's chug these last glasses and head out. We don't want to be too late, either."

"You're right. And if we don't see them, we will just party and get ratchet tonight."

"Bet. You know I'm down for a good ole ratchet time."

We hit the pen a couple of more times and finish off our glasses in the process. I have a great buzz, and Tia appears to have the same. I don't smoke too much these days, so it never takes much. We decide to catch a Lyft to the bar, just in case we end up really turning up, and because we are already a little fucked up. We sit back and enjoy the music our driver has chosen as we head to the bar.

The bar is about 20 minutes outside of where I live. I took notice of other businesses located on that strip while headed home that first night and just googled the street to find the place's exact location. I'm ok with directions, but I know I wouldn't have been able to get us here without getting lost if I didn't google it first. When I went to google it, I found a picture of it during the day, and it's called "Plateau." I had seen the name before but couldn't remember where. I went to the Facebook page to check it out. When I did, I saw how I knew the name. My new client, the fine older man Gabriel, owns this. 'On 22nd,' how could I forget that. I hope I don't see him here, especially not tonight, when things may get a little strange.

We arrive after what feels like the longest ride. Tia steps out of the car, and she is glowing. She's wearing a red, deep V-neck long sleeve body-con dress along with a pair of studded clear, pointed toe ankle booties. Her jewelry of choice tonight is a simple diamond bracelet, a diamond choker and a pair of large silver hooped earrings. Her hair is in its regular loose curls but pinned up in the back which draws more attention to her face. Her makeup is minimal and natural with a nude glossy lip. She looks amazing.

I opted to wear a dress from my spare bedroom. Xay had bought it and left it for me a few months back. I thought it was similar to what I woke up in that night at Plateau. It is a sleeveless sweetheart cut black latex dress. It stops right below my knees and has a split to mid-thigh. My makeup is my usual cat-eye, with a bold red lip. My shoes are a red tribal print pair of mules. All of this is a bit bold for my taste, but I'm really feeling myself in it, I can't lie. My body is popping, and my curves look killer. We both look so damn good. Tia takes out her phone and starts a Snapchat video.

"Ayeeee, and all my bitches bad. Especially my main one," she sings into the camera and then flashes it over to me. I smile, and we strike a sexy pose.

"Girl, you know these men are gone lose their mind over our fine asses tonight. Some of these hoes too. Whether we see them or not, we turning up."

"We look too good not to! But I hope I get some answers tonight."

We walk in, and both instantly get stared down. It's like every person in the bar stops to look at us. Compared to the people here, we're overdressed. Although, I think there's no such thing. We are, unquestionably, the best dressed here. I begin to scan the room, looking for Rocky or Gabe. I see a few familiar faces from the first time being here, but neither face is theirs. My anxiety is quickly ruining my high, I could use another drink; we walk towards the drink station in the center. On our way over, I hear two people say "Hey," and one even adds "Ryan" to the end. I ignore them and keep walking.

"This music is hitting. I wouldn't expect that from the looks of some of these people in here. Do you see them? What did you say they look like so I can be on the lookout too?" Tia squints her eyes and looks around the bar.

"No. I don't see either one. But it's ok. We can enjoy the scene for a while longer. According to their Facebook page, they have really good drinks."

I describe how they look as we wait for the bartender to come from the back. While waiting, a man walks up to me. I can hear Tia begin to call the bartender over as I shift my attention and body towards him.

"Damn. You look good as hell tonight. Are you feeling better now?" He looks me up and down from head to toe licking his lips.

"What? I don't know you. I'm good." I say as I try to

twist my chair back towards the bar.

"Oh, it's like that?" He stops my chair and twists it back towards him.

"I came here for one thing, really. You know where Rocky and Gabe are?"

" You don't know me, but asking about Gabe? He ain't here. Remember, you were mine first baby girl. And Rocky around here somewhere, you know she don't ever take off. You know you missing out; I can take care of you when you're done playing with thug toys."

He sounds so butt hurt. He looks alright–tall, heavy-build, light-skinned, nothing like my type. Gabe really isn't either, even with his looks. This is my first time seeing this man too. But I decide to play it cool to gather more information.

"First? I belong to no one. Don-" I feel Tia grab my chair.

"Excuse me, I need my friend." She smiles at the man and turns me back towards the bar. 'Looks like you could use a rescue," she whispers. I look up, and Rocky's walking towards us with drinks in her hand. She looks up and spots me.

"Oh, you got a new friend? Is that it? That's why you acted crazy and went M.I.A?" She holds her hands out, handing us our blue motherfuckers. Tia knows this is my favorite. I start to feel my anxiety kick in overtime and decide to chug it.

"So you just gone ignore me? What the hell you come in

here for? You know this is where I work, and you know I'm here every single night."

"Rocky, I'm not who you think. I was not acting crazy. I came here to clear things up for both of us. Or all of us, where is Gabe?"

"He's not here tonight. And what do you mean? Don't start with that Koni shit again."

"Girl, her name is Koni. You are the one who sounds deranged. Just hear my girl out before I have to get in your ass."

"Tia, be chill. It's cool," I say, raising my hand to silence her.

"So, you really don't remember me? None of the past two years?"

"No. This week was my first time ever seeing either of you in my life. I don't know this bar or any of the people. But you all know me? I'd like to figure out how. So please don't think I'm full of shit."

"Ryan, we...I mean Koni; that shit just isn't the same. We have had some of the best memories in the last year, and Gabe is in love with you. He even bought you a ring. He planned on proposing the night you wigged out. This is all a lot for us too."

"A ring? I just can't understand this. I don't even know when I'd ever have free time to see him. I have a whole man, a career. I'm a boring homebody. I'm just trying to make this make sense. Are you sure that the person you're talking about isn't just a doppelgänger?"

"Bitch, I'm sure. Shit, we have fucked before Ry. Several times, in fact, Gabe doesn't know. But I know it's you. You have a birthmark shaped like a hot wing on your inner right thigh. I can't believe you don't fucking remember."

Her eyes fill with tears, she looks like the very first time I saw her, only sad instead of worried this time. Her accent is starting to come out again as she gives me more details about every tattoo I have, about my belly piercing that I let close that most people would never know I had. She definitely knows me. I'm trying to make it all make sense, and I can't. Tia is looking at her crazy, but I can tell she just feels sorry for her. I feel bad for her too. It's obvious she's hurt by all of this.

"I'm sorry. I'm not trying to hurt you. I just came to understand myself. I think I have been having blackout episodes; it's the only thing I can think of to explain this."

"Black-outs? For two years? You're my best friend, Ry. I mean Koni. Or you were? You've never seemed crazy or off in any real way. I remember the first night you came in. You were alone, but when you walked in, the bar lit up baby. You came in and ordered a crown and coke, told me I was beautiful and asked where you could find a good stiff dick. I laughed and told you I'd had those types of days too. We hit it off from the first meeting. I've seen you at least three times a week since then. I can't believe you don't remember any of the shit we've gone through."

"Girl cut her some slack. You don't think this shit is scary for her too? We just came to see what the fuck was going on with this Ryan girl. I get it. This shit is new to you too, but I think you've guilted her enough for tonight," Tia says, placing her hand on my back.

My head is spinning. I'm trying to put together everything she has said. I can't understand how I can leave my house, come 20 minutes across town weekly, and not remember it or ever have a sign of anything until this week. I can't stand to hear anything else for tonight. I have to talk to Dr. Rainey before I go any further.

"Tia, it is new for her. She has the right to feel a certain way. I don't even know how I feel right now.' I pause, turning my attention back to Rocky. "Rocky, you have answered some things for me. I know I won't get all the answers tonight. I can't tell you that Ryan is gone, but I don't know how to make myself blackout. I can tell you that this is not the last you will see of me. I don't know the person you know. It's terrifying for me and honestly, just like for you, it's a lot to take in. Please tell Gabe to call me when he gets a chance. I'm assuming he has my number. We have to get home, but this will not be the last time you see me."

"Koni, I'm not sure if I want to see you again, to be honest. Figure out what the fuck is going on with you before you come back because this shit is crazy, and I can't deal. You don't answer the phone anyway. Everyone knows that about you," she rolls her eyes, turns her back, and begins taking the next drink order.

Tia follows me as I start to rush out of the bar. We schedule the Lyft pick-up and get the same driver who luckily decided to stay close. I can't breathe. I can't understand how this is possible. It's so much that doesn't make sense. Tia is quiet. I know she must think I'm bat shit crazy. She always has my back, but this is something new. I feel crazy as hell. Rocky proved that she knows me, or at least a part of me that I don't even know. There's no denying it.

"Are you ok?" Tia chimes in, unknowingly pulling me out of my impending anxiety attack. 'I know you're over there tripping. Honestly, I am too. But nothing could ever change my mind about you. Shit, I bet I've probably met her before, just thinking about things. With your moody ass. You're my best friend, I know this shit has to be scary but I'm here for you. Remember that."

"I love you," is all I can stand to muster. She leans in to give me a hug. I feel myself on the verge of tears. This is all too much. I don't know what I expected to hear tonight, but it wasn't this type of shit. I can't help but think about Xay. From what I heard tonight; I've been stepping out on him without even trying. I feel so bad; I would never cheat on him. He is my one. I can't believe I'm in this situation. Our Lyft pulls up, we both get in, and we're silent the entire ride home. He pulls into my driveway, and we thank him and get out of the car and watch as he drives away.

"I can stay over if you just need someone to bounce shit off right now. Or we can even go to a club depending on how you're feeling? It's completely up to you."

"I don't know if I can handle another social scene tonight if I'm honest. Sorry we didn't get to turn up."

"Girl, there is no need to apologize. Tonight has been a lot, so I get it. You want me to stay? We can have our own house party; I have enough weed and liquor for us both to be numb."

"No, I'm good. I appreciate you for coming with me. I don't know if I could've handled that alone."

"Ok, well as long as your cool. I'm about to head to Darius and have him make me numb instead," she laughs. "I will check in tomorrow. Please do not hesitate to call if you need me sooner."

"Wear that man out. Be safe and text me when you get there. Talk to you tomorrow."

She gets in her rental car and drives off. I walk in my condo, focusing on breathing tips I learned a while back from my therapist. My heart is racing, and my body is starting to feel like it's overheating. I feel like I can't catch my breath. My brain is saying that I will die if I don't breathe right.

I am in full panic mode. Tears begin to roll down my eyes, and I try not to scream. *Focus. Breathe.* I hate when these attacks come, I can never be rational in the moment. After 3 minutes of slow deep timed breaths, I finally start to calm down. I don't want to think anymore. I've beat myself up in every way, and I'm still confused.

I'm scared to have a conversation with Gabe after this. I don't know if I want to hear any more about Ryan. I'm also scared of what Dr. Rainey is going to say after she hears all of this. She's always so judgmental to be a therapist, that's why I always end up taking breaks from her. I'm eager to see her now more than ever though. Tuesday is not coming fast enough.

I decide against taking my prescribed medications just in case they have anything to do with the blackouts. I take a few sleeping pills to knock me out instead; I know my brain isn't going to shut down any other way. One good thing about tonight is that I didn't see Gabriel there. I have a big day of work ahead of me tomorrow and my second meeting with him is scheduled for noon. I need to be alert, and on my game, I don't want anything changing his mind about choosing me to handle his finances. The pills kick in faster than I thought they would. Thank God.

Chapter 4

I still feel groggy from last night. I overslept; damn sleeping pills. I'm finishing my makeup, getting prepared for the day. My phone begins to ring; it's Xay. I ignore it. I don't want him to hear anything off in my voice. I know that he'll just begin to worry. I'm still not quite ready to tell him what's going on. I don't quite understand myself. I know with the severity of this situation, it would be for the best just in case Ryan appears with him again. I text him instead, "Busy day baby, sorry headed to work early. I'll talk to you later. I love you. Have a good day." "I love you too baby," he responds immediately.

The negative effect this is having over me is apparent; my mental health is truly suffering. I rush to finish getting ready and arrive a few minutes late to work. The building is more quiet than usual. I don't have to make any cordial efforts. I'm happy because no one will notice I'm late. I walk in to see Shelly hugging some man while grabbing a container of food from his hand. She looks over at me, screams and jumps back. The man looks up and waves awkwardly.

"My bad, you scared me. I thought you were already in

the meeting and wasn't expecting anyone."

"Meeting? I don't have any clients scheduled until 11 today, according to my calendar."

"Yea, because all the advisors have a meeting this morning. I told you about this last week?"

"Last week? Shelly, you should've reminded me yesterday.' I roll my eyes. "I'm assuming it's in the conference room?"

"Yes, it is. And I'm sorry, I meant to send a reminder, I usually do."

"It's cool. I apologize, it's not your fault I'm late anyway. Can you start some coffee and bring it to the meeting? I have my smoothie, but I need caffeine right now."

"It sounds like you had a fun night. I know all about those mornings," she giggles.

"Oh, do you now? When do I get to see?" the man questioned while reaching out and placing his arms around her waist. She frowned as she picked his hands up and removed them from her waist.

"Hello? This is my job. This is my boss. You could've at least waited a minute. I'll catch up with you later, maybe. Thanks for the breakfast Key."

"Damn. Like that? Your conversation made me think-,"

"You weren't thinking. Obviously. Like I said, I'll hit you later." He lifts one eyebrow, nods his head and walks towards the elevator. She turns her attention back to me.

"Sorry about that. I really wanted him to leave anyway. I just wanted the breakfast girl. You know how that goes. He is on some boyfriend moves, and I don't belong to none of them."

"I was definitely wondering. I've seen you flirt with clients doing more than that," I say, shaking my head.

"One of these clients could wife me up any day now. Money talks to her different,' she slightly pats the front of her slacks and laughs. "I'll have your coffee to you shortly though. Enjoy the meeting." She heads towards the snack area to brew a fresh pot.

I walk over to the elevator and wait for it to come back up. By the time I get down to the conference room and get seated, Shelly brings my coffee, as requested.

"Now that we have everyone here," he pauses and looks over at me. "Let's get started," Ian, our CEO, says.

Asshole. I'm not that late for him to be so extra. The meeting is extensive. We discuss the company's statistics and how we compare to last year. Our services offered and our rate of pay is largely based on the clients we each have. The wealthier the clients are, the more they pay the firm. In the last year, I've maintained the same clients, adding very few new clients. However, most of my regular clients have had so much success in the last year, it has reflected on my salary and finally pushed me into the six-figure range.

The big bosses start to give out prizes and awards based on our personal metrics. I win an award for 'Most Success with Existing Clients' as well as 'Client's Favorite,' both come with $250 gift cards. Nicole looks at me with envy as I go up to accept them. As I walk back to my seat at the conference table, I stop and sit next to her instead. I lean in and begin to whisper to her as they continue to pass out awards.

"Don't worry too much. You're still new enough. I didn't win anything my first year here either. I was convinced these men didn't even know my name." I giggle, although it's true.

"Who said I was worried?" she asks as she looks up, cuts her eyes at me, and gives me a nasty scowl.

"I didn't mean any harm. It just seems like yo-, maybe I read the situation wrong. I was just trying to let you know you are not alone."

"I came into this world alone, and I'll leave the same. I don't need your help or fake friendship," she rolls her eyes.

"You're right. You won't have to worry about it again." I get up and walk back to my original seat. I don't know why I tried offering her any words of comfort anyway. This is one of the reasons I stay tucked away in my office. They conclude the meeting and provide a catered breakfast. I don't feel like socializing, so I grab a cream cheese pastry and orange juice and make my way back up to my office. I refill my coffee, go into my office and close the door. I thumb tack the awards to my wall collection from previous events. I scarf down my bagel, start my 'Chill Vibes' playlist and begin looking over Gabriel's expense folder. I'm anxious about seeing him again. I still can't find a way to thank him enough for the extra funds. I'd offer to take him out for a nice night in town, but I'd rather not send off the wrong impression. I get lost in my music when Shelly buzzes into the intercom system to interrupt.

"Koni, Gabriel couldn't make it, so he sent his son to the meeting. Is it ok if I send him back?"

Damn. I was looking forward to getting to look at him again. "Sure, Shelly, send him back."

I stand from my desk to greet his son with my hand extended. As I see him walking in, my hand drops right along with my mouth. It's Gabe, from the bar. What the fuck? I even took notice that they look alike; I don't know how I didn't put this together sooner. He looks just as shocked to see me but closes the door on his way in and proceeds to pick up my hand as it lies limp and shake.

"Ry, I been looking for you. Rocky told me you stopped by with a homegirl." He did a long silent pause. "I guess it ain't Ry? Or is it? This shit wild. My dad described you as a gorgeous piece of work. It would've been crazy if I had let him meet Ry, and he came in and met you instead. He's never even seen a picture of you. He would've thought you was on some setup shit. But little does he know."

I grab my hand back. "I'm sorry Gabe. I did try to see you. To try to put things together. Gabriel is your dad? Oh, is that why you were at the bar? You run that one for him?"

"Really, like you don't know this? Well, I guess you don't. Yea, he's my father but I don't really fuck with dude on any level but business. He ain't never here anyway. I just do him a solid by running the bar. Ryan already knows this. I've told him about you, but he stays gone so much he never has time for shit. All he gives a fuck about is money, but I don't really want to talk about him right now. So, um, Koni, can I ask you a question?' He pauses but doesn't give me a chance to respond before proceeding. "You really don't remember who I am or what we are to each other? Don't you remember our late nights and early mornings? Shit, even our fights? Some of this shit I could never get out of my head. I don't know how to feel. You look the same to me, but you are acting differently; I guess it's because you don't know me?"

"No. I don't. I'm sorry. I can honestly say I'm Koni and have no recollection of you until earlier this week. I don't know anything about your father but what he has told me. He did mention having an estranged relationship with his children. I'm sorry to hear that, but he seems to really care about changing that. I guess Ryan and I don't share the same memories. To be honest, this shit is wild to me too."

"Funny thing is, Ry recommended you, for finances. She said you are the best she knows, and you could handle all types of clients including someone like my father. The way she bragged on you, I should've known she was talking about herself." He starts laughing hysterically. I join in with the laughter involuntarily. His laughter comes to a sudden stop.

"I can't lose her, and I won't lose you. I'm not sure what's going on, but I'm here every step of the way," he pauses again. 'Koni, I'm Gabe. It's truly a pleasure to meet you." He stands back and holds his hand out. I shake it. He looks at me in the most admirable way. I can see the love in his eyes, and I don't even know him. I'm even more confused. I can't afford for him to think he has room in my life. I don't know what he means by he's not letting me go, he won't have a choice.

"Gabe, it's nice to meet you too. However, I do have a boyfriend. I'm having a real issue with trying to get over the fact that I've been fucking with you too. I didn't know what was going on; I had no control. But now that I do, you can't be here for me in the way you may be used to. I just need you to chill while I figure it all out. I'd even go so far as to ask if I, or Ryan, come back, for you to please avoid us at all costs."

"You didn't hear me the first time. I'm not going anywhere, and you better know damn well if Ry comes back, I'm never turning my back on her again."

"And if she never does?"

"She'll be back. She disappeared before. The only difference was I never knew about you and knew even less about her than I do now. I wasn't always good to her, so I just blamed it on that. Now everything is slowly making more sense. She is never available during the day; I thought she was just a workaholic. She rarely speaks on the phone and always refuses to text. Even the way your condo is set up; It's two bedrooms, and she has never let me see the second one. Weirdly, she has her own room when you say you didn't know she existed. I thought she was playing me with all that expensive shit in there. I knew she didn't buy all that shit just to use for herself. It's starting to make sense now. Even with all this crazy shit, I still want to marry her. I owe it to her to give her a chance to come back, no matter how we're going to do this. I can respect your boundaries as Koni, but I'm not going anywhere until I can ask Ryan myself."

"As long as you're respectful. I'm glad it's starting to make sense to someone because I'm still lost. The fact that you've been in my home? How the fuck didn't I notice something off earlier. I feel violated, but I can only blame myself. I'd rather skip the finance portion of the meeting if you don't mind. This has all been awkward enough. I have put together these reports; please give them to your father.

If he has any questions, have him contact me. I hope the next time I see you, it's on different terms. Have a great day Gabe." I hand him a folder with everything I planned to discuss today, walk to my door, and open it to let him out. He smiles.

"I'll leave you alone today, but it's not going to be that easy to get rid of me. I will see you soon, Koni." He takes the reports and walks out of the door.

I can't believe he's been in my house to an extent where he knows details. I can understand where he's coming from with not wanting to be shut out. This is new to all parties involved. I begin to have thoughts of Xay walking in seeing Gabe in my home. Xay has a key, what if Gabe has one too.

I feel my heart rate pick up drastically. I try to calm myself down while my mind attacks me. *Breathe. You're crazy. Remember to breathe.* I feel the tears rushing down my cheeks. *Breathe.* No one will want me after this. I'm going to lose Xay. *Please remember to breathe.*

I crawl under my desk and sit on the royal blue knit rug. I can't stop my body from shaking, nor can I stop the tears from flooding my face. *Breathe.* I don't want to take a pill, but controlled breathing isn't working today. I get away from under my desk, grab my keychain, and open the portable pill case on my key ring.

I always keep back up Zoloft and Klonapin in there for times like this. I pop a full Klonapin in my mouth, swallow and wait for it to kick in. It takes about seven minutes for my chest to feel like it isn't going to explode. My panic attacks are back and more severe than ever. I must tell Xay before this gets any more complicated.

❁❁❁

I'm laying down when the phone starts to ring. It's Tia. I answer, even though I wouldn't even usually be here right now, and I know damn well I shouldn't answer her call. It's not my place, but I feel like stirring shit up a little today.

"Hey, love! What are you up to today? Darius and I are free. You cool to meet?" I almost hang up on her. She's always calling on my time. I always ignore it because I never want her reporting back and because her damn voice can be so fucking annoying at times. Especially right now, I was browsing XNXX just about to play with my pussy since I'm apparently a gotdamn nun now.

"I'm not Koni." I say dry as hell. She begins to laugh, as I expected her silly ass to do.

"Well, who the hell are you today, bitch? Let me guess? I finally get to meet homegirl Ryan?" She begins to laugh uncontrollably–stupid bitch. I'm not her fucking homegirl.

"Tia, I already know you. But it is finally nice to talk to you, as myself." I lie and try to play nice.

"You play all day, bitch," she continues to laugh hysterically.

Chapter 5

It seems like everyone is all in my fucking business these days. I'm so sick of Koni and her boring ass. She's fucking up everything. My dick, my side pussy, my partying; all of it. Which is rude as fuck of her, especially considering I've managed to stay out of her way for the last 11 years. 17 years really but it was like I couldn't control shit the first six, so I never count them. I have stayed low key all this time; I haven't fucked with shit she has going. But as soon as this bitch sees a sign of me, she ruins everything. Now I feel the need to return the favor.

I would've never fucked Xay, but the way I'm set up, I need a good fuck session at least three times a week. She fucked up my appointments with Gabe, so I had to show her man what really fucking was about. Now, don't get me wrong, Koni can fuck, but she likes to usually play it safe and stick more along the lines of lovemaking. With one person. Where is the fun in that? It's better to have a variety.

Now that I've added Xay to my collection of variety, his ass can't get enough of me. If she worked with me instead of against me, I could really teach her how to keep his mind blown. His dick is good, and he really deserves better than what Koni can even phantom in her little prude bubble. He deserves pussy whenever and however he wants it. I really should've given him a test run years ago.

That night we went out was so damn fun. Koni was being her usual dry self, insisting that she wasn't going to drink too much. She had already forced me to be away from my man, getting fucked something proper, as I usually would be. She wasn't going to have me sober the entire night too. So, I waited until after her second glass of wine to make my grand appearance and show the fuck out. I ordered us a few shots and even lucked up on a motherfucker selling edibles in the club.

I usually wouldn't trust that shady shit, but since I didn't have time to prepare by bringing my own shit and Koni doesn't smoke like that to keep it on her, I took a chance. I overheard him trying to push some of his product off on two drunk women near the restroom; they weren't biting. They were looking for some cocaine or pills instead. I watched them get mad and storm off when he said he didn't have any drugs for 'crackheads.' I could understand why they'd think he sold it, by the way he looked, I would've bet money that he sold it all.

He had a total of four large free form locs with a neon green bandana tied around his forehead. His oversized ripped black and white Bob Marley sleeveless shirt accompanied by wide leg black trousers with heavy metal chains draping from each pocket reminded me of the shit the goth kids wore in high school. His clear platform sneakers didn't make the outfit any better, but I assumed by his look that he knew what good drugs were if nothing else. He had brownies, cookies, gummies, suckers, even chewing gum. That was something new to me, but I decided to stick to my usual brownie selection. I'm glad I did because they were extremely potent. I bought two, ate one in the club and saved the other for later. After about 25 minutes, I was high and drunk off my ass, feeling good and ready to fuck.

Xay has always been fine to me, even though Gabe is finer. I don't really have a preference when it comes to men, just give me all the fine niggas with good dick, I swear I'll show a bitch what to do with them. His song, *Drip Demeanor* by Missy Elliot blasted through the speakers in the club. He pulled me out on the dance floor to dance. Koni has a little more rhythm with music than me; all I know how to do is shake my ass as far as dancing goes. I grinded on his dick like I was at a high school dance, I felt his dick get hard, I kept going until my pussy was just wet enough.

When the song ended, I asked him to walk me to the restroom, acting as if I couldn't keep my balance. I love playing the helpless role; men love to feel needed. When we got to the restroom door, I pulled him in with me. He looked shocked and kept telling me how he knows I had to be drunk. I played my role and acted the part.

I unbuckled his belt, unfastened his jeans, and pulled his pretty dick out; I couldn't wait to get it in my mouth. He has a curve which only excited me more; it's my favorite type of dick to suck. I instructed him to fuck my face until he let me taste his nut on my lips. He seemed so hesitant, so I helped him out. I got on my knees and licked from his balls to the tip, took it all in until I gagged, spit on that shit, and repeated. I grabbed his hands and put them on the back of my head and kept pushing until he got the rhythm I was going for. I was sucking so good you could hear the pop every time he pulled my head back too far, and his dick came out my mouth. I made sure to gag while I looked in his eyes, just enough to stroke his ego.

I moaned and hummed on his dick so he could feel the vibrations from my throat. His legs started shaking after a minute and a half. Koni swears she stays putting it on him, but the motherfucker nutted in three minutes. He didn't follow instructions. He nutted in my mouth instead, which only turned me up more. I let him watch me play with his nut by letting it drip down the sides of my mouth and pulling it back in while looking in his eyes and playing with my pussy. His eyes lit up like I was doing magic.

I grabbed his hand, put it on one of my nipples, and told him to pinch hard. I've never been able to resist a quick nut from titty play. I came so hard while he watched in awe. I got up and made sure to get all the juices I could before pulling my hand from my pussy. I ran my fingers across his lips before putting them in his mouth for him to lick clean. I could no longer feel the slickness. He got every drop. He was so hypnotized, I felt like even more of that bitch than usual.

"Damn baby, you never sucked me like that before. You the best head I ever got...but tonight? This shit is the best you've ever done. And you being extra freaky. I'm loving this nasty shit. I need to get you drunk more often," he said while he pulled up his pants.

I felt some way that he thought I had to be drunk to suck dick good. Personally, the whole scene was almost basic. He was so hyped; I couldn't wait to get his ass home and show him what I really liked. We went back out and danced a little longer until I told him I was ready to go. When we got back to the condo, I insisted we go in my room. I'm more comfortable there.

That extravagant shit, that's all me. Even the shit Koni

thinks that Xay buys and leaves as gifts for her, that's all me. Men used to buy me shit often just for giving their whack asses a little conversation. Koni's crazy because she rarely questions anything. If it were me, I'd be all over it. She's smart as hell but can be so oblivious at times. Xay wanted to stick to fucking in Koni's room though, so I just grabbed a few of the toys I've been wanting to try with Gabe and met him in the room ass naked.

"Koni, baby, I love this drunk you," he was standing up naked stroking his dick.

"Call me, Ryan. Koni is no longer here tonight." I stared coldly.

He laughed and agreed to call me whatever I liked. Good, because I was tired of hearing him call me that. What the fuck kind of name is Koni? Sounds like an old white woman. The only thing I have in common with her is this fine ass body and face. The first toy I pulled out was a vibrating anal plug. It had a remote control that I gave to Xay and told him to buzz it every time I came. He followed instructions so well. The shit was better than a thumb in the ass while fucking. I came so fucking hard every single time.

He fucked me better than I ever expected. He got so excited when I squirted on his face. Really, he was excited over all my basic shit. By the time I got to riding his dick, taking the plug out my ass and putting it in his mouth while replacing it in my ass with his dick, he was losing his shit. He tried to grab some lube when he saw that I was about to ride it anally. I was offended and told him to shut the fuck up and let me make my own. My ass gets just as wet as my pussy does. He was even amazed by that.

I swear I felt like I was fucking a virgin at how inexperienced he was in certain areas. I always try to give Koni her privacy, but she's even more remedial than I thought. I came eight times in two hours. Even though he put it on me, Xay might as well had gone to sleep sucking his damn thumb. I had his ass whipped on the first night. His dick was even better than Gabe's, that's a hard task to accomplish. That curve made his dick fit perfectly, and his rhythm was on point. Gabe is way nastier, though. He matches my freak, so even though fucking Xay was fun, it only made me miss my man more. I'm going to get to his ass again, no matter what it takes.

Unlike Koni, I know that we share. I can control the switch. I used to just sit back until I was needed, which, with Koni, wasn't too often. She's extremely low drama, all about keeping the peace; until you push her, that is. Well, until you push us. But whenever it does come, it's nothing for me to show a motherfucker not to fuck with us.

Recently, I'd decided that I wanted to have a life too. Publicly that is. I found a good low-key vibe in that bar my first night out as myself. Most of those people were people that Koni was highly unlikely to meet. It was easy to build a presence there. Everything was low maintenance.

Both my friendship with Rocky and relationship with Gabe came easy. Even the other few randoms that I used to fuck with regularly throughout the last two years or so came easy. I never cared about any of them. For me, they were just something to get an itch off with. I didn't want them to fall for me. People have it bad falling in love with me, even with me constantly telling them and showing them that I'm not shit.

The first was Raquel. Others call her Rocky, but Raquel

has always sounded sexier to me. She was the first person I spoke to. I thought she was fine as hell from the very first time that I met her. I approached her on some friendship shit just in case she didn't like women. Once I peeped that she did, nothing stopped me from being all over her.

She's the best head I've ever gotten, both sexes included. She eats my pussy like it's her favorite meal. I've never had to ask. I can cum just by sucking on her titties, they are so damn pretty. She's the coolest bitch I've ever met. We're very similar; we like all the same shit.

I don't like relationships with women though, all she could ever be is just a friend that lets me fuck every blue moon. Sometimes I get that she wants to be more, that's what made me give Gabe a real chance. I figured seeing me in a steady relationship with a male would keep her from trying to build a relationship with me; it worked.

Of everyone, I instantly bonded with Gabe. He was really on some fuck boy shit, to the fullest, when I first met him. I didn't care. He was all on my row. He even stopped flirting with other women in the club to pursue me seriously. I told him when we first met that I spent my days working and taking care of my sick father, an excuse so that he would be more tolerant of not hearing from me often, also knowing he'd never find out the difference.

He just thinks I suck at communication, which is also true. I don't find the need to keep in constant contact with anyone in this state. I don't even make promises; I know that having to share means nothing is certain. Our setup doesn't allow me to be anything than what I am, as far as consistently communicating with others is concerned.

Gabe is the best thing that has happened to me, individually. He's sexy, assertive and goes after what he wants. He allows me to be open yet private in the ways that I need. He has his issues too; I never feel too crazy with him. He's the best thing I've had going with a male. I've stopped fucking around like I used to when I first got out on my own.

I used to take my frustration out with sex. I also really enjoy it. The control of it all is exhilarating. Gabe does everything I've ever wanted. Even put me on to new shit at times. He's older, so he has me more open than I've ever been with trying things. I've stopped searching for validation in others. He's taking me more seriously than anyone ever has. We've also had our rough times. At times, I was sure I let it ruin my idea of being happy.

For a short period of our relationship, he always wanted to fight. I kept it real with him on everything I could, honesty wasn't always best in our situation. I used to be a tease when I was only fucking with one person. Some people looked at it as cheating, but I didn't. I was only having conversations. Granted, some were deeper than others; it mostly meant nothing. I would seek validation in multiple areas; it was my way of socializing.

I never saw the wrong in it until I saw how Gabe would often react. Sometimes, I could sympathize and put myself in his shoes; most times, I couldn't. I never cheated while we were in a relationship, aside from this recent experiment with Xay. We had fun a few times with women from Plateau, and he knows about Raquel and approves. As long as I don't fuck or fall in love, it's nothing to talk to, or even sext, new prospects. He never has to worry. I never expected to still be at it with him. I have no need to censor anything about myself except the absolute necessity, of course. I learned with some people; secrets are better; I kept it too real.

The first time he left a mark, I had to disappear on him. It was a big ass bruise from punching me in my side. I couldn't have that happen to Koni; I wasn't that much fucked up about it for myself. Sometimes, I felt like I deserved it. I just knew that if I didn't put distance between us, he would've come up missing, putting his hands on me. I just chilled and let Koni live her full life again. It was boring as fuck. I'd only come out while she was asleep at that time. Never to do anything, maybe get a quick one-off, but nothing note-worthy. Things temporarily went back to what they were before I decided to live my life publicly.

Eventually, I went back–only after his over the top nonstop attempts. He'd send flowers to the condo during the daytime. Good thing he'd never leave a name. I'd see them on her dresser and notice the card just said, "I love you." I didn't know it was him until we were arguing one day, and he mentioned it. He'd stalk the condo from his car at night. I noticed him twice when I was headed out to meet up with Raquel. He even caught Koni out in public during the day once and tried to strike up a conversation. He thought Koni not acknowledging that she knew him was just me playing hard to get. It worked for me then.

I've done enough things to hurt him, including being downright disrespectful in some cases. Some shit he's just been sensitive about; I refuse to play anyone other than who I am in my time. He still loves me through all the toxic shit that is me and wasn't going to stop his attempts until I took him back. He was going to have this shit blow up before it did. He started to pop up at the condo during the day. Coincidently, every single time he'd pop up, we'd be away. He'd text me to tell me he was outside each time, but I'd never see it until much later. After getting the same text a week in a row, I decided to give him another chance. Although he is a little rough around the edges, overall, he is the perfect fit for me.

He hasn't hit me since we've been back together. He corrected my main issue with him, and we moved forward. He pretty much lives in Plateau. Day and night. I rarely interrupt Koni during the day, I've maintained only having to see him four times during the day since dating. Now that I've had a taste of being in control, I want nothing more than to make her disappear. Or at least make her dormant. I'm going to focus on getting back to Gabe first. I need to talk to him. I need to feel him right now. He's the only person that truly gets me.

Marrying Gabe, I'd have to make shit shake more in my favor as far as the time I'd get. I'd make more time for my husband, meaning I'd have to take more time, it's not just her body. I can live my life as Koni if my man still knows and loves me as Ryan. I plan to do just that. I had plans of telling him that night to make sure he still wanted to be around before putting a ring on my finger.

Knowing that Gabe now knows, and he still loves me, that's exactly why I will do whatever it takes to get back to him. He might talk shit, but he accepts me at all stages, just like I accept him. I have an entire routine on waiting for Koni to go into a sleep or relaxed state before taking over. It always has worked. The other night at the bar, I don't know how the fuck she came back.

That night was going to be so special for me. I knew Gabe was going to propose, despite the circumstances, I still fully planned on saying yes. It'd only give me more motivation to get rid of her sooner. Before she interrupted my schedule, I was content with how things were, too content to push for change. Even though everything is a mess, I'm thankful for the push Koni gave.

I dressed extra sexy that night and had my makeup done just for the occasion. The last thing I remember is talking to Rocky, asking her if I could eat her pussy under the bar while we waited for Gabe to get there. She tried telling me that I needed to behave and be considerate to Gabe. She doesn't know that I've already told Gabe that I've fucked her multiple times before and that I'd continue as long as she let me. She was looking so damn good in that little black skirt. I knew she didn't have any panties on, and I really wanted a taste. After promising to be quick, she agreed. I started to walk around the bar to get in position, and that's when I passed the fuck out.

Koni takes pills that help her chill out. I love them because although I feel them too, they aid in me being able to take control. She has less resistance when it's time for me to switch, and most importantly, she never remembers a thing. She has stopped taking her pills, so she's usually more aware these days, except today. She thinks seeing Dr. Rainey will help her again, but in reality, it will help me. I know she's going to try to bring me out, meaning I will be learning new techniques to take control.

I am looking forward to this visit just as much as Koni. I usually hate the visits. I'd even go so far as to call her psychiatrist mediocre at best. She never asks the right questions or researches enough for me to ever be interested in talking to her here. However, she may be able to offer help since she knows about me now. I will finally get to tell my side; I can't wait.

That night fucked up everything. She thinks I'm gone, but I'm so fucking tired of playing in the background, to someone like her, especially. I'm obviously the better choice to run this. If things were completely up to her, we'd never be where we are now. Now that she has ruined my fucking proposal and my life, that bitch has another thing coming. Two can play this game.

"Am I talking to Koni?" Tia sounded nervous, completely different than usual.

"Bitch? No. It's Ryan. Girl, what the fuck. What's up?"

"Ok. I don't know how it works. If you can, tell Koni to call me. Leave a note to yourself or something," she says like she's about to hang up.

"Girl, you know I'm joking. It's me, Koni, what's up with you?" I question, beginning to worry about her.

"Koni? Bitchhh, I'm glad it's you! Girl, I spoke to Ryan," she says, back in her usual peppy tone.

"What? When did this happen? Was it today?" --my voice begins to fade out at the thought. She, well I --I talked to my best friend as a part of me that I don't know and can't remember.

"Girl, yesterday! I called last night after you got off because Darius and I were free, and I wanted you to meet him if you were up to it. You answered as Ryan. I thought you were playing at first, so I just kept laughing. Her tone was different than yours, but I didn't catch it in the beginning. She sounds like she hates me. She's dry as hell. She got annoyed with my laughing and went into a rant about not being able to fuck and being frustrated. I tried asking why she was there, and she told me she didn't have time for my bullshit and hung up. I tried calling back. I called until your phone started going to voicemail last night. I'm glad you answered this morning."

"Please tell me you're joking," I try to scramble for any memory from last night.

"I wish I was. That Ryan is something else."

My mouth might as well be on the damn floor. I wonder what triggers her. I took a nap when I got home yesterday. My medicine had me feeling groggy. The pill. That's probably the trigger. I thought I just slept through the night. I can't have my man, my friend, or my life to myself. I'm staying in for the rest of the weekend. I'm not taking any pills; no matter how bad these anxiety attacks hit, I will stay up all night if I have to. I should've scheduled an emergency visit and had them hospitalize me if necessary, at least then, I'd be monitored and safe.

Chapter 6

I told Xay I was sick over the weekend, so he gave me my space. He insisted on bringing over the illness essentials, but I told him not to and promised to make it up to him this week. I know he's feeling some type of way because I have been neglecting and avoiding him for a week now. Today is the day. I finally plan on talking after my appointment. I ignored everyone and didn't get much rest in the last few days.

Yesterday was the first time I'd called out from work in a while. I called out again today. I feel like I'm losing control of myself. It scares me to the point of just wanting constant seclusion. I don't know what I'm expecting out of this meeting with Dr. Rainey today. Being honest, I hope she has an instant cure to get rid of all things that aren't genuinely me, but I'm sure it won't go anything like that.

My appointment is today at noon. I feel like I should also be looking up banishing spells and figuring out how to conjure them correctly. I'm open to all options. Just in case it's a bad spirit hanging on, I sage my home to cleanse all negativity. I try meditating in hopes that I can connect with her. None of this seems to be making much of a difference in my mood or mindset, but I'm still trying to make sure I'll be able to say no stone went unturned. After trying everything I can think of, I head over to her office.

"It's been a long time Koni." Dr. Rainey says as she comes to greet me by placing her hand on my shoulders. She's dressed gorgeously, as usual. She has on a black pant suit. The blazer is fitted but wide at the bottom. The pants were fitted and straight legged. Her heels were thick and low. She wore them well. Her skin is some of the prettiest I've ever seen.

I chose her because I wanted a black woman, and she was one of the closest to me. I feel that having someone the same skin color is important they could relate a little more to some of my struggles. She walks me towards her emerald couch. It complements the love seat and the soft gold walls in her office. She eloquently strides over, takes a seat on the love seat and begins pulling a few materials from a small black chest she has sitting next to it.

She has classy taste; it's obvious by her setup. One wall has all of her degrees and certifications. She's been in school her entire life, according to this wall. Her office looks the same as usual, small and chicly decorated. There's minimal furniture. The only thing that has noticeably changed is the addition of an area for children with toys, games and stuffed animals. It's always been so welcoming. After looking around, I can tell she's waiting for me to say something, I gather my thoughts and give her my full attention.

"It has been a long time, Doctor. I thought I was doing good, and I no longer needed to talk my issues out, but here

I am again."

"Well, what brings you in today? What would you like to talk about?"

"I really don't know what to say. There's another me, would be the only way that I can describe it. Her name is Ryan, and I just became aware of her last week. I woke up one night in a bar I'd never been with people I didn't know. Since then, everything has been unbelievable. I feel like I'm losing control. And I need help."

"Hm. Ryan. Ok, we'll come back to her. What do you mean by losing control? Tell me exactly what happened," she starts to scribble in her notebook.

I begin to give her the quick version of what has happened up to date. She surprisingly doesn't interject or say anything to indicate that she's judging me. She asks the basic questions about what I know about Ryan and how long I've noticed her. She seems extremely interested. Thinking back on it, I had my first blackout moment in college with my boyfriend at the time.

I remember we were fighting but can't really remember the specifics, we always fought. Well, he always fought me. He reached out and struck me in my mouth, I remember the rage building inside of me, and my brain completely shut down. I woke up to him one step from trying to kill me, claiming I had smashed an aluminum can against his face causing the deep red scratches on his cheek. I swore he was lying; I'd never take it that far. I believed I hit him because the scratches came from somewhere, but that story was extreme. Nothing could've ever convinced me it happened, until this very moment.

I quickly start to realize she's been here much longer than I care to admit. She's someone I've always brushed off as anger issues or drinking issues. She's named herself, which successfully made her presence too loud for me to continue to ignore. Dr. Rainey's first series of questions help put together a lot for me. We talk for a while. There is no doubt in my mind that Ryan is real. She diagnoses me with a new title, Dissociative Identity Disorder. She picks up a purple book with enough words on the cover, but all I see is DSM-5 before she opens the book and begins to read the definition for clarification.

"Dissociative Identity Disorder; disruption of identity characterized by two or more distinct personality states or an experience of possession," she pauses and puts down the book. "Unfortunately, there isn't a 'cure' for this one. There are a few methods we can try, but this will not be an overnight process. I know how much you hate talk therapy; however, coming to terms with this will require a lot of talk therapy. Please hear me out on this, I feel that after the last nine years of knowing you, this diagnosis explains you best. We had pieces missing from the puzzle, we still do. But now we get to work on the real thing."

"Ok. But she's coming around more and more. How do I stop that for now? I can't just talk and not see results. I need real help now."

"There is no off button. It doesn't work like that. In this case, I'd suggest you let her come as often as she'd like. You need to figure her out. She needs to be seen by those close in your life because it sounds like whether you like it or not, she's here to stay."

"What? Let her come? That's your advice? I've been waiting a week, for this? No. Fuck no. This is my life. Why would I give it up for someone else? Man, I should've gone to someone else," I hiss as I begin to stand up and walk towards the door.

"Koni, you are my girl, but you're my client first, do what's best for you. Most, if not all, doctors will tell you the best way is to learn to cohabit with Ryan. Meaning, never stop her if you're able to control it. You said you believe your medicine enhanced her taking over? I'm going to ask you to stay off all of them for now. We'll try to bring her out to talk naturally. We need you both to co-exist and become one. This will take some time. I'm giving you homework," she pauses as if she's waiting for my acceptance. I pause at the door and roll my eyes. She takes it as a sign to continue. "Write down every blackout you can remember being told about or any time you've woken up in an unfamiliar location. I need you to document your feelings in-depth and bring them back to your next session. The instant outcome that you are looking for is non-existent, but I can ensure you'll be better off with this resolution."

"I'm here for all of it. I'm even a step ahead by not taking the medication. I just don't know where to begin as far as organizing it all. How do I start making more sense of all of this? I know the homework may help you, but thinking back on the little I can remember, it truly scares the living shit out of me. I don't know who she is, and I'm not sure I want to. I just thought I'd leave with more clarity."

"We are just getting to know of Ryan, which still leaves much to be imagined about her. You now know where to begin. I can't stress enough that this truly will take some time. I want to see you twice a week. Are you able to fit me into your schedule?"

"I don't think I can afford not to. I need help sorting

through all of this, and I'm trusting you. I don't know who to tell and who not to. I don't know the next time she may appear. I'm scared of what else could go wrong. I know our hour is up so, I'll schedule upfront and talk to you later in the week."

"Don't forget, you can always call me anytime you feel overwhelmed, or just need to talk about anything. I'm you're listening, but most importantly, confidential ear. And remember homework, homework. See you later, Koni."

I walk out of her office heading to the front to schedule my next two appointments. I feel somewhat of a relief from speaking to her. It actually feels like it may have helped. It gave me the space to think it out; I've never gotten that way with Dr. Rainey before. She usually makes me feel like she has never made a mistake in her life, yet this time she seemed understanding and helpful. It wasn't a complete waste, after all.

I get back home and decide to take some more time for myself. I start on the homework immediately. There are so many things coming to mind that have been here all along. I can't believe she's been around for so long. Having to ransack my memories sheds light on so many things. College was weird. I always blamed any blackouts on excessive drinking or getting too high with my friends. I barely remember her and very little of anything else if I'm honest.

The times I remember as blackouts, I don't. They are called blackouts for a reason. I scribble down a few things as different memories pop up. One memory, in particular, stands apart from the others—one where a man called me Ryan, all the way back in college. I didn't think about it earlier because I thought he had called me the wrong name.

It was college, and after a night that I thought I got blackout drunk because I didn't remember anything the next morning. I woke up to him giving me the best head I had ever had at that point in my life. I was embarrassed because I didn't recognize the man in any way, but I was letting him get well acquainted with my pussy. I had no choice but to cream all over his face. He moaned as I wrapped my legs around tighter and came even more. He was trying to say something, but I wouldn't let him catch his breath. This was the closest I had ever come to a one-night stand, and what he was doing felt so good I decided to live in the moment for once. He grabbed my cheeks and pushed me harder against his face. He put me down and pulled his big thick pretty dick out, put a condom on, and was positioning me in that 'have my baby' position, pinned down with my ankles at my ears missionary, as he was about to stick his dick in.

"Ryan, you wanna be a freak so bad. Ride this dick, and prove it," grabbing a fistful of my hair as he thrust into my pussy. I wigged out. I pushed him out of me so fast, pulled loose of his grip on my hair and hopped off the bed.

"You can at least have the courtesy to get my name right. Rude ass," I say as I scan the room for my anything that looks like it belonged to me.

"Ryan? You don't have to make any excuses. I thought we were having fun. My bad, I'll call you whatever, whenever", he says, still lying in bed naked.

"You think this shit is cool because we're just fucking, huh? I don't know what girl you have me mixed up with, but you are so disrespectful," I yelled as I quickly got dressed and gathered my purse. "Too bad you'll never taste me again; you were doing a pretty decent job for a stranger.

And a tip before I leave, just leave names out completely. I would've rode your face until I made you cum. Leave it to a man to mess up a wet dream."

He began pleading his case, telling me how I told him that's what my name was and that I needed some type of mental help. At the moment, I thought he was lying. I didn't care because I didn't know him to care. I was just offended by the audacity. I left and never saw him again. I didn't even know the man's name. So, no loss on my end. I feel guilty now. Like I owe him an apology, if I knew him, I'd reach out.

I begin to think about who else I could've done this to throughout my life. Nothing is coming to me now. My attention drifts to Xay. I'm not looking forward to this conversation. I'm supposed to meet up with him, and I'm running late. I get up and rush out the door to head to his loft.

He lives about 15 minutes away from me. It takes me no time to get there. I use my key to let myself in. I can smell his cologne greet me as I enter. His loft is so beautiful. I've thought about moving in several times, but I don't want to get tired of him or vice versa. I see him coming out of the bathroom, looking like he just took a shower, glistening. I walk up and hug him. He kisses me on the lips and asks how my day has been.

"Hey, baby. I know I've been a little distant lately, and I feel like I owe you an explanation." I pause and take a deep breath. "I went to see Dr. Rainey today."

"You good? Thought you were done with therapy? You haven't seen her since college."

"Yes and no. I thought I was done too. I've had a few

things happen in the last week that I've dealt with alone, as not to worry those close to me. Especially you."

"Baby, you could've talked to me. You can talk to me about anything. I thought you knew that."

"I do, but I didn't know what exactly to say. If I'm honest, I still don't know how to say it, but I guess I'll just come on out with it. I have another personality that I recently met, and you've apparently already met her too."

His deep baritone laugh echoes around the room. "Baby, if that's what you're worried about, I can testify that you definitely have about five of you. Most women do; you are perfectly normal. Now come here, you were talking like I was going to lose you or something crazy." He pulls me in close, wraps his strong arms around me and kisses me on the forehead. I pull away slowly and look directly in his eyes,

"You might." His smile fades quickly. I continue.

'Her name is Ryan. That night you thanked me; It wasn't me. I don't remember anything about that night after my first drink."

"What? We role-played that night. You always get nasty when drinking. You don't remember any of it? Probably because you were really wasted. You drank more than I've ever seen you drink."

"I tried to blame it on drinking too. It's not drinking. I woke up in a bar surrounded by strangers who have known me as Ryan for the last two years. I don't know all the details, but since that night, it doesn't seem like she's in hiding anymore, and I don't know how to make her."

Silence takes over the room. I can see the questions forming by his facial expression, yet, he says nothing.

"She's been around for an exceptionally long time. I'm not exactly sure when she first got here but dissecting my memories, I'd guess it's been longer than you."

"How? H-h-how have I never met her or heard of her until this week? You've never used the name before. Are you sure?"

"I am sure. I wish it weren't true."

"Well, what about the people in the bar? Do you know them? Have you seen them since? I'm sorry if I'm asking a lot of shit. This is hard to take in."

"Trust me, I know. I'm struggling myself. I want things to stay the same with us, but I understand this is a lot to ask of anyone. Please listen with an open mind."

I begin to catch him up. I want to give him a choice of whether he can deal with this or not. I tell him about Rocky, Gabe, Gabriel, about going back to the bar and everything uncovered in therapy today. I need him to understand the severity of the situation. Telling him about Gabe was the most painful. I watched as he tried to control every thought about how far I had gone with him.

"Do you know if you've been fucking him? Do you, or Ryan love him?"

"I have not fucked anyone except you, and I don't know him; there is absolutely no love there. I honestly can't speak for Ryan. That'll be something you have to ask her if you get another chance."

I can't tell him that I know Ryan has fucked Gabe or Rocky. I can't hurt him any more than what this situation already will. I will not lose Xay to someone I don't even know.

"Koni, baby, I love you. You know I do. I'm ready to spend the rest of my life with you. I've told you a million times; you are my one baby. I can't and won't share you though. I will be here for you throughout this if you continue to choose me and only me."

"I will always choose you."

He wraps his arms back around me. Tears roll down my cheeks and hit his yellow button-down, my mascara staining his shirt. I pull away and open my mouth to apologize; he places his finger over my lips.

"Baby, it will be ok. We will be ok; you are no longer in this alone. We are the team. We will conquer this, just like we do everything else. I love you, girl."

"I love you Xay," I say through clenched teeth trying to stop myself from breaking into tears again. I couldn't imagine my life with Xay anymore. Every dream I planned has changed. I can't imagine our future. At least he knows now. I should've told him earlier. I feel like at least a portion of the world has been lifted from my shoulders.

I used to keep a separate phone when I first started testing the waters to see what I could get away with. I figured eventually she'd discover the phone in my bedroom, so I did away with it. Now I just use this app called Burner instead. It's in plain sight, and she has so many unused apps on that phone that she's never even noticed. The app gives me a separate number and a certain amount of texts and minutes for calls. It also has the option to hide notifications. That's been the best for this situation. That way, my life doesn't interfere with hers. I set all of this up out of respect, and she still goes and tries to shut my shit down. Nothing will keep me from getting to fuck my favorite person.

Gabe made me change my habits. When I first fully got out into the world as myself, I was a bit promiscuous. If I'm completely honest, I came out to play a couple of times in college too, but it was a rare occasion. I remember coming out once, going back to a guy's house I met at a party when Koni had too much to drink and being so bored with him and his dick that I checked out to let Koni handle him. It was fun fucking with her head and funny that she talked bad to his ass for calling her the wrong name. He was more her speed when it came to sex anyway.

I was sick of Koni's choice in men and had too much frustration built up from dealing with them. Xay was the first decent man she ever met; he was part of the reason that I did not fully come out as myself earlier than I chose to. Koni has always been so reserved sexually; I needed something different until I met Gabe. Now I am exclusive with Gabe and girls we bring in to have extra fun. Raquel hits my taste for pussy when I don't feel like auditioning a new girl to join Gabe and I. Between fucking them both, I haven't needed another dick or pussy.

All week I've had to rely on self-play to really get me off, and that hasn't been good enough. I switch, just to reach out to Gabe and ask him to come over as soon as Koni falls asleep. He's excited to hear from me; It's all in his voice. I'm happy she decided to come back home and not sleep at Xay's tonight. He gets here in less than 10 minutes. I open the door before he can knock. He's walking up to my driveway when I see him. He's wearing a pair of loosely fitted light wash denim jeans, a black sweatshirt with the words "Billionaire Boys Club" printed on the front in large letters with a pair of tennis ball neon green colored Foamposites to compliment the color of the letters on his shirt. He always dresses so sexy. It's nothing like a guy with a nice hood swag. I can't help but admire him as I close the door behind him. I take his hand and begin to lead him to the bedroom. He mentions something about Koni, and I immediately cut him off.

"I know everything that you are about to tell me. I am always here, even when you are speaking to Koni. I'm not like her. I've missed you, Daddy. The bitch has deprived me of my favorite drug. You. I need it right now. We can talk later." I lift my dress and bend over to expose my pussy to Gabe in a sexy lace crotchless bodysuit. He leans in to kiss my butt cheek. I lift back up and give him a look of disgust.

"No one gave you permission to put your dirty lips on my pretty ass. Get naked now. I'll tell you when and what you can taste, do you understand?"

"Oh, so this what you on tonight?' He smirks and begins to undress. 'Yes, Ma'am. I understand."

He loves when I do my dominatrix shit. It's been almost two weeks since the last time I've gotten to fuck my man. I want every ounce of control tonight. I start walking towards the bed, raise my finger and motion him to come to me. He walks over with his dick swinging. It's erect already; he has the sexiest grin on his face. His strides are powerful. He knows he's the shit, and that turns me on.

"Where are your fucking manners? Apologize to me."

"I'm sorry. I should've asked for permission first. Can I eat your pussy as an apology?"

"To apologize? You were going to do that anyway. Now, we just have to do it 100% my way."

"You know I'm down to please you. In every way you like. Use my face as you like," he says as he gets to his knees beside the bed. I lift one leg off the floor and prop it up on the bed.

"You take orders from me. Not the other way around. Don't make me have to punish you more than I already plan to. Smell my pussy. Put your face in it and inhale, but you better not lick it."

He leans in to obey. His lips line up perfectly with my clit. As he inhales deeply, I push his face harder into my pussy.

"Do it again and jack that dick while you're doing it. It's begging for attention."

Again, he says nothing and obeys. I pull his head away from my pussy, spit on his dick, and push his face back in it.

"I'll let you lick it if you ask nicely."

"I need to taste that sweet pussy. I miss it so much. Please, let me suck on that fat thang until you squirt on my face," sounding muffled, I can feel every word on my pussy.

"Good boy! Taste this nasty pussy, and you better make me squirt nasty too."

He stops jacking his dick and moves his hands up to spread my pussy lips open. He sticks his tongue in it to get all the juices I've already created. He smears it all over his face and moves up to my clit. He begins to suck on it slowly. I slide over onto the bed to get comfortable.

He stays on the floor, pulls my ass to the edge of the bed, pushes both legs back and continues to suck slowly on my clit. I begin to moan. With his skills, he could easily finish me in two minutes, but he always takes his time. I'm on the verge of cumming already. My legs begin to shake, and I can no longer control my moans. My thighs close in on his face. He pulls his head away, comes up, and begins to fondle both nipples as he stares in my eyes.

"Can I make you cum right now? Or should I make you wait?"

"I want to see your face soaked. Make my pussy squirt right now." I push his head back in my pussy. He sucks on my clit while fondling both nipples. I scream. I can't contain myself. I cum once, and it squirts out a little.

"You're so fucking nasty," I scream as I try to catch my breath. 'Put your dick in this wet pussy. Make me squirt all over that dick."

He gets up quickly and flips me over into doggy style position. He starts to pound my pussy while pulling my hair with one hand and choking me with the other.

"So. Fucking. Nasty. I can't take this dick. It's too good. It's too good. I cannn't," I scream as I begin to feel myself squirt on his dick. He chokes me harder as he feels it squirting out onto his legs. He's fucking me so hard I can't breathe. I can't control the squirting; it just keeps coming. I tap the bed because I can't seem to make out any more words. Gabe continues to fuck my pussy hard. The slapping of skin and my screams echo through the room until I black-out from the choking and pounding. I wake up right in time to catch him pulling out, flipping me over, and shooting his warm cum all over my face as I gasp for air. He moans and collapses on the bed. He rolls over and kisses me on my shoulder.

"Damn Ry, I didn't know if I'd ever get this pussy again. I missed you so damn much girl," he begins to caress my stomach.

"I know you did. I watched your effort, and it has had me determined to get back to you. No one compares to you."

"You could've told me what was going on. I'm never giving up on us, baby. I hope you know I mean it."

"I know baby. You've shown it. I usually can maintain control, but I don't know what happened that night at the bar. I planned on telling you everything that night, and suddenly I couldn't keep control. I'm trying to figure out how to keep it for good now. Because of you, I'll never give up either. Koni has no idea what she's up against."

"Never? That's what I needed to hear. I planned this a little differently, but shit went wild that night," he says as he gets up, grabs his pants from the floor, and goes searching through his pants pockets. He pulls something out and clenches it in his fist tightly then begins to lower to one knee. He opens his hand to showcase a red box with the prettiest ring I've ever seen enclosed. It had a dainty onyx band with an exceptionally large, princess cut, beautiful black diamond. It's far from ordinary and precisely along the lines of what I've always wanted.

"Ry, I am fully in love with you. I know I could've waited with things being so crazy right now, but I can't risk losing the opportunity forever. Ryan, baby, marry me!" he says as he extends the red box. His eyes are glossy, holding back tears.

"You know I will marry you, baby. We will make this work, if we keep fighting for each other," I can hardly get my words out. He takes the ring from its box and slides it on my ring finger, it fits perfectly. I jump up into his arms and kiss him on the lips repeatedly. He stands there, holding me and smiling. I have a man determined to marry me, something I thought would never be possible.

Chapter 7

"You've been different lately. What's gotten into you? Or should I say who?" Shelly laughs as she grabs one of the yellow tulips Xay had delivered yesterday. "You and hubs tried something new? Where are those tips I keep asking you for?"

"If I had any real tips, I wouldn't hold out on you. I keep telling you I got blessed with this one."

"You just being stingy. I'm trying to get a glow like yours. We can share him if you are ever in the market of looking for a third," she winks at me and bursts into laughter. I know she's serious. Xay would probably like her too. He has a thing for screwing ghetto girls; he says they are the freakiest. I'd never invite her to join us because she can't keep a secret. I'm too discreet to chance it.

"Thanks for the offer Shelly, I'll be sure to file that away," I say sarcastically and roll my eyes.

"I'm just kidding, boss lady. I forgot you can't take a joke. He is fine, but I don't steal anything that doesn't come to me."

"Good to know. When is my next appointment? Noon?"

"2 o'clock, with Gabriel. Mr. Lee rescheduled for next week."

"Shoot. I forgot about my appointment with Gabriel today. I need to go over a few things to prepare for our meeting. Could you send over that spreadsheet and pull any other clients that I have today? Once you're done with that you can take an extended lunch, just be back to remind me 15 minutes before Gabriel's appointment."

"Great! Will do. I appreciate you, boss," she cuts the conversation short and heads back to the front. I knew that would get her to leave me alone. I start to look over the spreadsheet for Gabriel's finances. He is making way more than expected in every business. He's making some of the smartest investments I've ever seen; I should take a tip or two from him on how I can do the same.

It's been about a week and a half since my first session with Dr. Rainey; I just completed my third yesterday. Therapy is so helpful for piecing things together, especially when I'm lost on where to start. I believe Ryan has been with me since college now. I've blacked out at different times since then due to anger. I never know what happens during those times, only what others tell or show me when I come back. Dr. Rainey believes that there is no reason to fear Ryan because she stemmed from the need for protection. She said people sometimes create other personas to deal with different traumas, so it makes sense.

My life has been in complete disarray. Xay seems enthralled that there is someone else to get to know. He's been trying to be around more. He's been asking more questions about Ryan. Sometimes it feels like I'm in therapy with the type of things he asks. If I had to guess, I'd say it's solely to get to talk to Ryan whenever she decides to come back. He has been very accepting; I don't know why I didn't tell him sooner.

As far as I know, she hasn't been back since the Tia situation. That's only as far as I know. Gabe has popped up here twice in the last week. He's been acting weirder than when I met him. He even asked me about why I wasn't wearing a ring and asked what I did with it. I don't know what ring he's talking about because I don't have one and haven't seen him since the last meeting in my office. Everyone handles loss differently, so I'm trying to be nice.

Rocky mentioned that he was supposed to propose that night, but he seems to have completely lost it. I feel the love he has for Ryan will never go away, so I may have to put distance in between us slowly. He has gotten flowers delivered to Ryan twice as well. Both times security sent them up just assuming they were from Xay and never checked the card. I've already told security not to let him up moving forward; it's scary for him to keep popping up. It's like he's obsessed with me. Or Ryan. I may just be paranoid, but it's been too many strange coincidences occurring at once. Shelly buzzes in.

"Koni, there is a Raquel here to see you. She's not on the appointment schedule, do you have time to meet with her?"

Raquel. It has to be Rocky.

"Walk her back please," I say, holding the button. Shelly walks into my office with Rocky close on her heels.

"Ok, I'm headed out now, I'll be back before your next appointment. Would you like me to leave the door open?" she asks with a look of suspicion on her face.

"No, you can close it on your way out. Thank you, Shelly."

She walks out and closes the door. Rocky is standing there as if she's waiting on me to say something. She's wearing a blue crop hoodie, a pair of high waist jeans with a pair of grey Yeezys. She's very casual and isn't wearing makeup like the previous times I've seen her; she is still incredibly beautiful.

"What brings you here, Rocky?"

"Gabe told me where you work since Ryan never shared anything real about herself. He also told me to mention that security will no longer let him visit. I had to come visit you for myself because I still need more answers," drawing her oversized bag closer to her as she looked around the room.

"Gabe can't keep popping up here. This is my money; I don't need any extra scenes happening while with my clients. But, off of him. I may not have the answers you're looking for."

"Well, he did finally give y-,' she rolls her eyes and clears her throat, 'Ryan the ring. What'd you expect of your fiancé?" she asks sarcastically with a smug look on her face. "I want to see Ryan. I know that if he can make her come back, so can I."

"Gave it to Ryan? When? He mentioned a ring, but I brushed it off as him having a difficult time coping. When did this happen? To my knowledge, she hasn't been back in the last week or so."

"About a week now, I think. He said he went over to your place and asked her, and she said yes. The ring was really nice; I saw it myself."

"Where is the ring now? How did he get in my home? Does he have a key? I'm sorry, I didn't know. I can't just make her come back, hell I don't even know when she comes."

"I don't know the answers to any of that, and that's not what I came for. I can't help but feel a certain way that she hasn't contacted me. I guess it shows where I really stand with you." Tears roll down her eyes, "I know, it's not your fault. I'm just not ready to let her go. I love her."

"I'm sorry, I don't mean any harm, but now is not a good time Rocky. I can't help you. Thank you for stopping by. Would you mind not popping up here? I can't have the risk of anything that I can't control happening here. I'm sorry."

"Damn. I can't come by either? How do I get in contact with you? You, well, Ryan never answers and rarely ever called back. Or do you just propose I forget about Ryan completely? That's not going to happen."

I can't focus on her and her meltdown right now. At this point, I wish everyone just could forget about Ryan, including me. This is all becoming more drama than it's worth.

"I don't know what number you have because your number isn't in my phone. In fact, no extra numbers are. I've never gotten a call asking for Ryan, so I don't know what's up with that. I'm not telling you to forget her. I'm willing to meet with you later. I just need more time to process things. You seem like a cool person. A good friend to have."

"Later when? Ryan is my best friend, and if you're going to pull the same shit that you're tryin' to pull on Gabe, I deserve to say goodbye at least."

"I'm not. I just can't have this at my job. I'll meet you at the bar later if you're working tonight?"

"Ry....I work every night. What's a good number, just in case you pull a disappearing act?"

I reluctantly give her my number and compare it to the phone number she has. I've never seen the number she has for Ryan. She saves my number in her phone and begins to call in front of me. My phone starts to vibrate; she peeks over at it to confirm her number popped up.

"Please save mine. You can't get rid of me as easily as you think. See you tonight," she eyes me from my head to toe and shakes her head. I stare back at her; there is nothing more I can say. I watch as she leaves. I'm looking for the same type of answers she's looking for; too bad I can't talk to Ryan myself.

I don't have any strange texts, calls, or contacts in my phone; I checked the first time she mentioned Ryan never answering at the bar. If she had a phone, it'd have to be somewhere at home. I'll have to look around when I go today. If Gabe proposed there without me knowing, anything is possible. Ryan has been back, and I can't begin to pinpoint how or when. What I'm doing is not working, I'm not finding answers. I come up with the idea of having cameras installed around the house and possibly in the office, just in case. Seeing it with my own eyes will help me figure out a way to get rid of her for good.

Her presence hasn't affected my work life, which I am thankful for. It's about the only thing. If Shelly ever gets to meet her, she'll have a field day; I'd never hear the end of it. I call around to get quotes on setting up a home camera system in my downtime and remember that Xay is handy with all the tech things. I begin to call him and then hang up. I don't want him to be concerned any more than he already is. I also want to see how he interacts with her if she comes back, to expose true intentions.

After calling six companies, I backtrack to the company that quoted me the cheapest, which wasn't very cheap at all, and schedule an appointment for installation. They'll be out tomorrow, the sooner, the better. As I'm finalizing the details of the appointment, I hear Shelly laughing at something in the lobby. I look at my clock, and she's back right on time. I'm waiting for her to bust in my door to let me know she's back like she usually does but she doesn't. I just keep hearing her laughs get louder. I get up to see what she could possibly be out there laughing at so hard. I walk into the lobby, and there she is standing with her ass backed into Gabriel's crotch while he is squeezing her waist and nibbling at her neck from behind. Neither of them notices me standing there, so I clear my throat.

"Oh, Hey, boss lady! I'm sorry I meant to tell you I was back, I got a little distracted," pulling away from Gabriel and straightening out her hair and dress.

"It doesn't look like that's the only thing you forgot to mention," side-eying her. 'Gabriel, you're early."

"It's good to see you, Koni. I thought I might as well head this way since I was free earlier than I thought I would be. And if you don't mind me being blunt, it doesn't hurt that you have this beautiful assistant. I could wait here all day." He winks at Shelly, and she starts to blush.

"It doesn't look like Shelly minds, so neither do I. If you're ready, we can go ahead and get started."

He shakes his head in a yes motion and begins to walk towards my office door. He's dressed just as nice as the first time I met him. He's wearing a pair of khaki tailored trousers, a Gucci blazer, with a black turtleneck on under. He paired it with Gucci loafers and his camel-colored briefcase. I follow him into my office and roll my eyes on the way in, so Shelly knows that I don't find this behavior acceptable at work.

"So, Mr. Grove, how have you been?"

"Please, call me Gabriel. I've been living the dream sweetheart. I apologize if the display with Shelly was inappropriate, it was all me; I hope I didn't get her in any trouble."

"Not at all. She's a good woman and an even better employee. We're all adults here, I know sometimes we just get caught up in the moment. You are fine. Now on to business. Your investments seem to be producing well above what was projected. I'm honestly blown away by these numbers."

"Yea, those numbers don't matter. I'm trying to be legit but old relationships won't allow me. I just want to be done with it all."

"Done? With all the businesses? You've brought in over nine million in just this month alone. What man in his right mind wants to throw that away? I wanted to know if you had any investment opportunities or any stock available in any of your current businesses you run. These numbers motivate me to branch out more than my usual."

"Koni, don't. Just stay out of this shit," he says with a calm tone, but with obvious agitation. "I told you I am working to get legit. Do you know how I became in charge of so many businesses? It's a service I offer to my clients. They need a way to hide the excess money coming in from their, uh, not so legit hustles. I offer them fronts disguised as investments. Those numbers don't mean shit, except that my clients are doing well for themselves, which will only draw a red flag to me."

"What? Like laundering? So, these businesses aren't even real?"

"Oh no, they do actually exist. What's taking place in each one, though? I can't speak freely about it. I need help to get out. Some of them are extremely dangerous people, and I don't need their shit pouring over to my family. I've already funneled some of their money through my bar. Honestly, it's the only reason I opened that bar. Did you see the numbers for it this month? Do you think people are actually in there, drinking that much?"

He looks stressed, but I can't help but get caught up in how breathtaking he is, still.

"We need this shit. This is our chance." I hear a voice in my head. I realize that I've zoned out completely, I see his

lips stop moving, and I pick up right on queue.

"Relax. It's nothing we can't come up with a solution for. You told me upfront you needed my help to get legit. I didn't know what that check was for, but now I understand. I'm still glad you chose me. Have you talked to the owners? We need them to distribute the money a lot different to stay out of the IRS radar because with them comes so much more."

"Take the fucking opportunity. Take it; we need this. Think about your dreams. Easy money. Just listen to me for once." The voice is becoming louder. I may need to take this opportunity; it will get me so much closer to owning my own everything. I try to focus on Gabriel instead of my thoughts.

"Believe me, I know. I feel like someone has already been watching me, but my partna's say I'm paranoid. I'm sorry to get you involved in this. You're too fine for any of this. And you're involved with my son, right? He wouldn't tell me any details, but after I sent him in place of me for the last meeting, I knew something had to be up. You must've not known he was my son?"

"It's ok, really it is. As far as your son and I? It's complicated, and I didn't know he was your son. I don't mix business with personal affairs."

"He's been talking about you for the past year or so. I just never knew it then. I've never met any of his old girls because he doesn't fuck with me as I mentioned earlier. He didn't tell me much, but the little that he did? You must be one amazing woman to make my son want marriage. I've never heard him even mention the word before last year. After meeting you, I agree, you are something special."

"Well, thank you. However, I will not be marrying your son anytime soon. I met him under difficult circumstances, and now I have to get him out of my life, I just have to work on my approach because he isn't taking it well. I'm serious about not mixing business. Not to be short, but we were discussing ways to get you out of this. Are you interested at all in keeping whatever it is that your clients pay you?"

"Get him out? Oh, I don't think he plans on leaving your life any time soon. I don't want any of it anymore. Some of them will accept that I no longer want to be in this game; others won't let it go that easily. They think I have too much leverage over them. Believe me, I've already tested the waters."

"Ok, so we just have to come up with a way to wash your hands of this life completely. You have a pretty nice savings and could live comfortably off it for the rest of your life. I must be honest, I've dealt with clients who have not been legit, but the laundering is something new for me, I am open to any suggestions you may have from the streets view. If you trust me, I can work with your clients if you are done? I would advise reaching out and telling them you will be getting out of the game due to personal or health concerns. Tell them you have someone who can help provide the same type of services and explain my background in finances. It'd get you out of your jam and allow me to quit this firm and start my own."

"Koni, I can't let you do that. I can't let you act like Captain save a hoe to come to my rescue. Some of these people are more dangerous than you could imagine. I think I may have a solution that helps you get rid of Gabe and helps me in the long run, if you're serious?"

"Can't? I am simply offering a solution that will help us

both. It isn't just to save you. When you gave me that envelope the first day, I was ready for whatever you threw my way. I know a way to handle this without anyone getting caught up. I have so many clients and access to many different businesses. I can stretch this money in ways you couldn't imagine. I wish I knew what I was up against from the beginning; it would've never gotten to this point."

"Even more reason I could use your help. You have the skillset to design a certain story on paper. This idea will help you get rid of your problem and mine as well. Just like your solution to take on my type of work."

"How do you propose I go about helping you while getting rid of Gabe? I am not trying to hurt your son in any way, I just want him out of my life."

"I didn't want to scare you away on the first meet, but I feel like you're ready now. I don't know what's going on with you two, but I will get rid of him, and he won't be harmed physically. It will need to be done today. Are you sure this is a move you are willing to take on? I don't want to have you in a fucked up situation. If you've never been locked up before, it's nothing to be played with."

He doesn't know that he has come in and given me exactly the move I need to start my own. Up until today, I thought I made the wrong decision choosing a 9 to 5. Now I can finally do everything I want, with incredibly low risk and get rid of Gabe all in one move. One less problem I'll have to worry about. This is truly a win-win situation for me.

"Gabriel, I'm far smarter than you are giving credit for. Finances are my expertise. I'm used to helping clients hide their money and assets from their spouses and family; this is right up my alley. We'll go over the details of getting Gabe to leave later, but I am in. I will take care of your problems, and you can help rid me of mine. We met for a reason."

"Ok, Koni, this will be a huge help if they agree. If this gets me away from this world, I wouldn't be able to thank you enough. I will not get caught back up in the system. Although something in my gut is telling me it may already be too late."

"Don't say that. Speak positivity over your life. It is handled. Now, go have those conversations, and when you give me the ok, I will come running. If this goes as planned, I truly won't be able to thank you enough."

"No wonder why that boy wants to marry you. You're smart, fine, and have a side of you that I wouldn't have guessed existed." He smiles at me, walks towards me and extends his hand.

"A side that no one does," I laugh and shake his hand. He passes me an envelope of things that need to be switched out of his name, and a few documents that need to be doctored up today. It also includes instructions to place an anonymous phone call in 2 hours from a burner phone he has included.

He lets himself out. This couldn't have been any more perfect. I'll be able to push Gabe out of my life and be able to afford the lifestyle I've been working so hard to achieve. I decide to be nosey and get all in Shelly's business for once. I walk out and see her smiling from ear to ear.

"So, you and Gabriel?" I raise an eyebrow and place my hand on my hip as I shift my body weight to one side.

"Girl, you're just as surprised as I am. We were coming to the building at the same time, and I thought I saw him checking me out. So, you know I put a little more sway in my hips. He mentioned noticing me the first time he visited and how he'd love to take me out if it's allowed. Girl, you know I was sold. And before you get to nagging, he started it, not me. But I told you if he bites, I was biting back. Rich and fine as fuck? Sorry boss lady, I couldn't pass this one up."

"It's ok, Shelly. We have something in the works, and if it goes correctly, he won't be my client on that level anymore, and I don't care what you all do at that point. Just don't fuck up before this deal hits for me, please?!"

"Fuck up?', she scoffs. 'Girl that fine motherfucker better not fuck up his chance to get this! I dreamt about his fine ass, look at me manifesting.", she waves an imaginary wand and starts to laugh. I laugh with her. She does look especially striking today, the neon yellow dress she's sporting goes so well with her skin tone.

"Well, when you do let him have it, I want a review on if it's as good as it looks," I giggle to myself, "I'm just playing. Any woman can appreciate a man that fine is all."

"Oweee, you nasty girl. Let me find out you a freak outside this work persona. Owww," she says in full Cardi B form. I laugh and roll my eyes.

The rest of the day goes by quickly. I speed home thinking about the phone that must be there. Once I arrive, I begin to search the house in its entirety. I call the number that Rocky had to see if I can hear any ringing or buzzing. It has to be here. I don't hear anything. It may be silent. I search my room, no luck; then I begin to search the spare bedroom. The phone is nowhere to be found. It doesn't make sense for her to have a phone, because who would be footing the bill? Gabe? Possibly.

As I'm searching the spare bedroom, I notice a male watch. Usually, I'd think it was Xay's, but he only has two watches that I've ever seen him wear, and this one doesn't fit his style at all. It's big, flashy and digital. I pick it up and put it away in one of the drawers. The first drawer I open is full of toys that Xay and I have never tried; everything opened and appearing to have been previously used. I also find a nice size bag of marijuana, a metal grinder with a ying and yang symbol on the front and a pack of Raw papers.

I'm upset at the number of people that could've been in my home. The thought of her possibly smoking really fucks with my head too. I used to smoke back in college and quit to build myself and my career. I felt it was holding me back and out of my budget. Although it's back in my budget, we have a random policy at work, I would've bet everything I own that I had clean pee. A couple of times with Tia wouldn't have the same impact as smoking however often she does. I've never so much as smelled it in the condo. I'm so ready to get these cameras installed, I can't take not knowing what's going on in my own home and more importantly, with my own body.

I pour myself a glass of wine to try to distract myself. I decide to roll a joint of her stash to calm down; nothing else seems to be working right now. I grind it up and roll a perfect joint. Not too bad considering it's been years since I've rolled one. I spark it up and try to let my mind drift off. I know! I need to talk to Tia; she always gets my head right. I pick up my phone,

"Hey Siri, call Tia!", holding my phone up to my mouth as if it's a microphone.

"Calling Tia, pink heart, green dress", Siri chimes back. It's always funny to hear her pronounce the emojis.

"Hey sugar, are you busy?"

"Sugar? Girl, are you high? Hell, are you Ryan?" she questions. I imagine her dramatically rolling her eyes and huffing into the phone. I start laughing because she always knows.

"Well, yes I am. High. Not Ryan. I'm smoking as we speak, but I completely fucking deserve it."

"Why are you high? When did you start smoking again? I thought you only did it socially now? Who the fuck have you been social with? I'm back in town, why didn't you invite me?" she questioned, finally pausing for a response.

"Woah woah. Slow your roll, girl. It's Ryan's. Apparently, my fucking spare bedroom is her room now, I found it in there. And bitch when did you get back and why wasn't I your first call?", I take another puff from the joint and begin coughing.

"I literally just got off my flight 30 minutes ago. It was a surprise to me too. Darius is throwing some fancy-ass event and wants me to be there to show off. And girl, what the fuck are you talking about? Are you drunk too?"

"Ugh. I've had one glass of wine, no I'm not drunk. I just wanted to vent. Today was fucking weird, on multiple levels."

"Ok, well get to it. I want to hear what happened to make you hit a joint by yourself."

I hear a call coming in on my phone, I pull the phone away from my face to look at the phone.

"Really?"

"Yes, it's me Face Timing you, answer! I need to see this!"

I accept the FaceTime. Tia is in the backseat of a car Darius sent to pick her up, she's extremely casual, no makeup with her hair wrapped in a satin pink turban. I start to tell her about Rocky coming to my job, about what she said about Gabe, the whole offer with Gabriel, and finding this shit in my spare bedroom. I can't believe I'm saying any of this.

"Honestly, I'm putting a lot of shit together still. Do you know how many times I've gone in that room and seen clothes I've never worn or bought, food and shit left out, just weird things in general? I've been brushing it off this whole time as Xay just using it, but it's been her the whole time. I'm going bat shit crazy because she is really me."

"Girl! You needed a fucking joint after what you've been through today. This bitch got a man to propose to her, even in these circumstances. Bitch, I'm tryna see what this girl got going?! Then, you are about to be rich as fuck, and I'm completely here for the white-collar crime shit," she laughs as she begins to flick an invisible stack of money towards me.

"Not white-collar crime shit." I laugh. "I hate you so

much." I begin dancing for the invisible money.

"Girl, this shit is the craziest shit I've ever heard. Would you like some company? Or to get out and come to Darius'? You two can finally meet face to face, and it may help distract you?"

"I do need to meet him before you leave this time, but I can't find it in me to be social tonight. I am mentally exhausted. When are you leaving out?"

"I honestly don't know. I'm thinking maybe sometime next week, so it's ok. You'll have plenty of time."

"Ok, well, I will get with you this weekend. I'm supposed to be going back to the bar tonight to meet Rocky, but I really don't feel like the shit."

"I think you should go, even if it's just to tell the bitch to fuck off. Do you want me to come with you again? Darius and I don't have anything planned tonight."

"No, it's ok. He flew you back out, enjoy your man girl! I'll go, but I'm not staying long at all. I can't really do anything for her anyway because she wants to speak to Ryan."

"Still go. But ok, I'm about to try some new shit on his ass tonight."

"New shit? Ohh, what you trying girl? I might need to take a few pointers since Ryan out here putting my man on some new things."

"Oh girl, it's nothing really wild. I've already tried that grapefruit shit on him, and he loved it. You might judge me for this one, but you know I don't give a fuck. I want him to come in my ass, and I make it come back out. It's called an anal cream pie, I think. We watched porn together a while back, and it was something he seemed really into. I kinda been practicing,' she pauses as she begins to wave her hand in a dismissive motion, 'don't ask me how."

"Bitch, what kind of freak shit?' I start to laugh. 'Ok then, give him the show of his life."

"You mean what kind of porn star shit. Put some respect on my name," she laughs. "And you know I will. Call me and let me know how everything goes. Be safe, and don't you dare hesitate to call if you need me." She hangs up.

I change out of my work clothes into something a bit more casual. I throw on a pair of jeans and a cropped pastel blue and white windbreaker jacket. I slip into some pastel pink lace-up heeled booties. It's perfect for tonight. I decide to take my car this time since it's only 20 mins away. I don't drink because I'm driving, but I do have an edible that Tia had delivered to me last week. I don't partake much, but with everything that's going on, I appreciate having something to take the edge off. I eat it before I start my drive because they take about thirty minutes to kick in, and the timing will be perfect.

I pull up to the club and immediately peep something is off. There is no loud music that you can hear outside. The valet isn't in the front like he was the previous visits. I see two parked police cars outside with the lights flashing but decide to brush it off as typical club atmosphere on a Friday night. I get a good spot near the entrance and head inside. No one is at the entrance to let me in, check my I.D, check my bag or whatever it is that they are supposed to do. I walk right in and see all the lights on, where it's usually pretty dim. People are standing along the walls, all looking toward the center of the room, I stop in my tracks as I follow their stares.

I see a total of four policemen. Two are busy off harassing some of the patrons, and the other two have a man hemmed up in cuffs pushing his head down. He was dressed like a typical hood guy in the club. A short-sleeved plain black t-shirt, a pair of fitted jeans sagging a little with a Gucci belt, clearly just for decoration. They begin walking in my direction. Their voices echo as they begin to read him his rights. My first instinct is to move, but I want to be nosey and see if I can get a glimpse. I stay. They get so close; I can smell one of the officers is wearing one of my favorite scents for men; Sauvage by Dior. Xay wears it all the time; it has me ready to melt every time I get a whiff. Just as I'm opening my mouth to compliment his cologne, they jerk the man's head up right before walking out the door.

"Gabe!" I reach out towards the officers. He peers his eyes my way, lowers his head, and begins to shake it in a motion of disappointment.

I look at the officers and begin to cry, "He's my husband. Can I please just say goodbye? Please!" not knowing why I was saying that. He isn't my husband.

They both pause and look me up and down. I give my best pretty pout in a begging motion.

"Alright, honey. One minute," one of the officers says in a thick southern accent, which I'm not used to hearing in Washington. It reminds me of home. He releases his grip on Gabe and backs away a little. I hug Gabe tightly and lean in and whisper.

"What for?"

"They say laundering and some other shit. But I swear I didn't do shit. It's a setup."

I put my finger over his lips and hug him tighter. He pulls me back and looks into my eyes.

"Ryan, I knew I chose right. I love you, baby," he says and leans in for a kiss. I pull back and fiercely shake my head. I don't know what I'm doing.

"I'm not Ryan. I'm Koni." I'm horrified myself. He looks at me, confused. I'm looking the same. Before he can say another word, the officers interrupt.

"All right, break it up, break it up. Sorry missy, he's gotta come with us now," the same officer with the accent says. He grabs his arms, pushes his head back down and walks him out the door.

Chapter 8

I don't know what that was this past weekend with this bitch and my man. I tried to take over, but I couldn't. I don't know why because she was in her right mind. It was almost like she wanted to hug and kiss him too. It was her first instinct to yell his name too. My fiancée is in jail, and I couldn't even spend that last minute with him. I switched as soon as he was escorted out of that door. I've been here ever since.

I'm doing what's necessary to protect myself because Koni has no regard for me or anything that belongs to me. I've been having so much fun as Koni. Unlike her, I let people in her life believe my name is whatever they want it to be. I got the pleasure of speaking to Tia again, this time I really gave her a piece of my mind. It's not that I hate her, she's just fucking annoying. She will not stop blowing the phone up. I think she's a little slow because she's still trying to be my friend.

It's crazy how accepting Xay is to this entire situation. He likes sitting around and just listening to me talk, even when I'm saying crazy shit. Even when I'm talking about

Gabe. He doesn't care; he's so wrapped up in who I am, I can't help but feel more interested than ever. I told him if he ever mentioned me taking over that he'd never see me again. He's been quiet ever since. He won't mention it to Koni, and that loyalty is rare. It's not cheating if he's technically fucking her body. I've fucked him maybe four times. It's fun fucking him because he gets to cheat without cheating. He's way nastier than he ever let on, and I can see why any woman would want him. He has good conversation, and he's genuinely a good man. He's stern still, and it's sexy.

I've been feeling a way about him, but I have always respected her relationships, so I've abstained. I could easily act like her or be her at all times if I wanted. That's just extremely exhausting. I don't like people, I don't like interacting honestly, but I will if I have to. When I have to. Xay told me what makes me specifically beautiful and what sets me aside from Koni to him. I'm bold. I'm confident, demanding and free of others' opinions. He even asks about me when I'm not around. I can tell, he cares about me too.

I called out today, but the last few days in the office have been a big ego boost. I love Shelly. She's fun and ghetto. She's fine as fuck, and I'd let her use my face as a seat any day. Those dresses she wears are so damn sexy; I've even masturbated thinking about getting to shove her face in my pussy in the office. She can tell I've been openly flirting with her this week. I've complimented everything about her, hinted that I've been curious to try women for quite some time. That's only a half-truth. I know if I told her at any moment to come lick it, she would. All her clients seem to like how down to earth I am as well. They keep mentioning how nice it is to see me loosened up for a change. I'm touching everything I can touch in her life right now. I need her to feel what she's doing to me. But also, show her that

I'm better at everything, including being her.

Raquel's phone number begins to flash across the phone, I answer on the first ring. She's called the burner number a few times since the first bar incident but always at the wrong time. I'm glad to see she's still thinking about me. I've missed her.

"Koni, this is..."

"Raquel! Girl, it's really you!" I say in a high-pitched tone, excited to hear that sexy voice of hers.

"Ryan?! Is this you? Ryan?? I thought I'd never talk to you again!" she says, sounding shocked that I answered.

"Never think that. This shit is just really complicated. I've barely gotten the chance to see Gabe, but now I have more freedom than before. You will be seeing me more. Koni will be out for a while."

"Out? How? I still don't understand any of this. Are you saying that you can control when you show up? How does that work?"

"Yes, I can mostly control it. I've always known about both of us. It's just Koni that can't, and just recently learned of my existence."

"Girl?! Well, why didn't you tell me? We've shared everything else I can think of! But something like this? The shit doesn't just slip your mind. I thought you were my best friend?"

"Rocky, you know we are more than that. You are mine. I don't care about anything else you or I have going.

You're mine. I didn't want to hurt you. I wanted to slowly get rid of her on my own terms, things just took a turn for the worst that night at the bar."

"I was starting to feel bad. You didn't reach out to me. I needed you just like everyone else Ry."

"I'm sorry. You can come over if you want. Do you remember how to get to my house? You've only been over here once if I recall right, so I can drop the location if need be?"

"You changed my world that night I was there; I'll never forget how to get there. I'm about to be on my way."

"Oh, is that right? That night was on some next level shit. We'll talk more when you get here sexy."

"See you soon, Ry."

We hang up the phone. I start to freshen up myself, and the house. I slip into a black lace and satin, mostly sheer robe, and slide into a pair of black fur slides. Raquel has always been vocal about her feelings. She's very direct. I do love her too, although she thinks I do a shitty job at showing it. I have to admit, I could do a better job, but I still show it. She shows me love from a woman that I've never received before. She lets me have my cake and eat it too. We've had some wild nights. She's fun, funny, territorial and a down ass friend. She never judges, and she's always ready to ride. A knock on the door interrupts my thoughts. It's her; I let her in. She's just as beautiful as always. She has on some high-waist black satin pants with a low deep v-cut top. Her body is perfect. She begins to shake her head and frown her face up as she looks me up and down.

"Damn, just like that, huh? You didn't even think we were going to have to talk first?"

"I wasn't trying to offend you. I just assumed we were ok from the call." I grab at the robe and try closing it more.

"Not at all. I pretty much already mourned you. I needed closure on this chapter of us. I'd like to keep the friendship portion open for whenever I can see you, if that's okay."

"What do you mean? I told you I'm here for a while. I have to be careful and think about how her life affects me too. I haven't been able to keep up my same schedule out of respect and necessity. But right now, I really don't give a fuck. I missed you."

"But you still didn't reach out to me. You say you can control it. A call would've been fine Ry. You don't go as hard for me, and I'm done with that. This is the last time I'll give you the chance to choose me last; I'm really too dope for that."

"What? I haven't been with anyone besides Gabe. I haven't spoken to anyone; you know I rarely use the phone anyway. That hasn't changed. I haven't had as much opportunity to see you. Don't be like this. I'm only able to control under certain conditions, and I finally figured it out. Gabe is in jail too, and I've been stressing over it. I've tried calling him several times since, and he hasn't answered. The jail won't give me any information."

"He's out. His father posted his bond, of course. He can't see you right now. When I was calling, it was for Koni. He has some crazy shit going in his head. He thinks Koni set him up. He said his Dad was telling him something about their last meeting going favorably for her. But since she stopped him from popping up at her job, he thinks she has it out for him."

"No, this was not us. That career move was beneficial for both of us. And I know I'm crazy, but I'm not on that type of shit for Gabe. Koni didn't do this. I'm worried about him. He finally proposed like you said he would. The ring is beautiful." I flash my finger for her to get a good look at it in person. 'I would never do or allow anything in my control to happen to my future."

"Well, his Dad tried telling him he felt something was up before you but he's just on his shit right now. This isn't what I came for though. I know you care about me, but you're just selfish. Call me when you're on some reciprocity shit. It was good seeing you, though. Until next time," she says as she lets herself out the front door.

Damn. I was hoping to get some bomb head, but it wasn't all of what she was making it. I really do miss her. She's so emotional sometimes, it's really the only thing I don't like about her. She'll get over it, she always does. She did mess my head up with that shit about Gabe. This whole situation is crazy, but I can see how it wouldn't be too farfetched of him to believe. I'm hurt that he hasn't been answering my calls since he's out, but I understand why. I will find a way to get to him.

Koni has therapy today, I'm really looking forward to wreaking havoc and finally meeting Dr. Rainey as myself. The phone starts to ring again; it's Tia. She's going to keep calling until she can speak to Koni, and I'm ready to give her ass a show.

"Hey, girl? What's up?"

"Koni?"

"Yes, girl. Again, with this shit? Have you spoken to Ryan again or something?" I say trying to sound as clueless as possible.

"Girlllll. This shit is getting out of hand. Ryan really doesn't like me. I've been trying to get in touch with you for days this time! I even tried your job. You must be off to-day?"

"Days? Girl what? I've been here the whole time, and yes, I took off today because I have therapy. This shit is scary, and therapy is not working. I want the bitch gone for good, this 'talk it out' shit isn't doing anything." I add to sound more convincing.

"I thought you said it was helping. It's not anymore? I think you should still go to your session today. Therapy is never an easy process. To be fair, I've only spoken to her twice, that's not too bad. Bitch, I'm starting to take her dis-gust for me personal. Like damn, what did I do to you, girl?"

"Now you know damn well. Don't take it personal, I have no control over what she says or does," I say, knowing she really doesn't. This is fun.

"Ok, well, I was just calling to see if you were free to go to the event, I mentioned earlier that Darius invited me to? Apparently, he's going to be busy hosting and suggested that I bring a friend. I thought it'd be a nice opportunity to distract your mind from all this bullshit."

"Oh, I definitely need the distraction. My mind is just

not here for it today. I'd love to attend, when is it?"

"It starts at 7:30 p.m. tonight. I have three dresses for the occasion; I'm going to have one sent to you since it's such late notice unless you have one in mind? It's a formal event."

"No, I don't. Send me one over. This gives me something to do tonight, and I finally get to meet the man in the flesh."

"Girl, I swear he looks just as good in person too," she laughs, and I fake laugh right along with her.

"Girl, don't stress yourself too much in the meantime. Thank you for agreeing to come with me. I don't want to be around all his snobby ass friends and colleagues alone. I'll come by to get you around 7."

"Ok, I'll be ready by then. I can't wait," I say, thinking if only she knew.

Chapter 9

Freshly showered, I throw on some sweats and an oversized t-shirt. Since I'll have to put energy into getting ready later tonight, there's no need to go through it twice. Grabbing the keys on the way out the door, I make my way to the therapy appointment. As I'm pulling into the parking lot, I spot Dr. Rainey getting out of her car. Her wine-colored fitted pant-suit paired with a basic white fitted shirt is hugging her petite thick frame perfectly, it is complemented by a sequined navy oversized clutch and navy pumps. The wind slightly beats against her beautiful straight ginger hair as she walks toward the office. Her cocoa skin is glowing.

I must be her first appointment of the day. She isn't looking up, so she doesn't see me. I've been looking forward to this appointment, but now that I'm here, I don't want to go in. I try to focus on small details about Koni to be mindful to stay in character when I go in here. After about 10 minutes, I get out of the car and go inside to check-in. I see the front desk lady; she doesn't see me. I knock on the plastic divider twice before she acknowledges me. She slides the divider open.

"Who are you here to see?"

"Dr. Rainey," I answer. She begins to type something on her keyboard and confirms what comes up on the monitor.

"Koni Reese at 4?", she asks looking up at me over her glasses. I shake my head up and down.

"Have a seat; I'll let her know you're here and she'll call you back in a few," closing the divider before she can get the last word out. I turn back to the lobby. I see one Latina lady in the lobby with a child, and no one else. I begin a game with myself, throwing around the possibilities of what brought her here as I pick out a magazine to flip through. She calls me back before I'm able to take a seat.

"Welcome back, Koni. What would you like to talk about today?" she asks as she makes herself comfortable in her plush velvet blue love seat. I begin to shift on the matching couch to ease my smart-ass mouth and keep what I'm thinking to myself.

"I don't know where to begin, really. This week has been a wild one," trying to mimic Koni's tone.

"Ok, well, what made it so wild? Has Ryan appeared again?"

"Yes, or so I've been told. Raquel came to my job this week to see her. She mentioned me not allowing Gabe to come visit and something about him proposing to Ryan last week. I haven't seen a ring anywhere, and I've searched extensively. I don't understand how Ryan is still able to have a life without me."

"That does sound like a pretty eventful week for her. How does it make you feel knowing that she has not gone away but instead is still attempting to live out whatever she has in mind? It's a pretty big step for her to be able to accept a proposal."

"How does it make me feel? Really? Terrified. Here I am coming to you in hopes of getting rid of her, and it seems as if it's making her...stronger," unconsciously smirking.

"Well, you are saying terrified, but your body language says something different. It's not a bad thing that she is coming up more often. I told you the goal here was to bring her out so that you can learn to live with her, and ultimately gain control over both personalities."

"I've just finally become at ease enough with it all. I'll never have control over Ryan. No one ever will."

"Is it still happening to where you don't remember any details of what you were doing when she took over? I know sometimes, it's possible to know the two exist and to be able to watch as yourself but not interact."

"Once last weekend. It was strange. Gabe went to jail for money laundering, and I walked in as they were taking him away. I was there. I could see, hear and feel everything, but I couldn't respond," I answer. I still don't know what the hell happened that night.

"And if you could've responded, what would it have been?"

"It would've been the same thing that she said to him. She stole my last minute with him. My last words."

"Your last minute? With Gabe? Did something happen with you two that I missed? The last you mentioned him, you were telling security not to let him up. Did you have a change of heart?"

"No, nothing changed."

"Very short. Ok, we can come back to it later if you prefer. Why were you at the bar?"

"I went to meet with Raquel. After she popped up at my job, I requested that she leave, but she gave push back. I agreed to meet with her later at the bar, and when I went, the police were already there."

"So, did you see Rocky at all?"

"No, I didn't get a chance. I blacked out after the Gabe incident."

"How long did the blackout last? If you had to guess."

"I don't know, maybe a few hours," I respond getting frustrated. "I really don't care to talk about that night anymore."

"Why were you upset with Koni for stealing your last minute?"

"Because I just needed to say good-bye, she didn't."

"Interesting. Are you feeling overwhelmed? Having any suicidal thoughts?"

"Do suicidal thoughts include getting my body to myself? If it does, I have them every day."

"Not necessarily. I don't believe you would cause physical harm to yourself. Killing someone off mentally is normal. But in your case, you will not get rid of her. We must change your thoughts. It sounds like we may be in for more drama, and the first thing you need to do is accept that there is another part to you. You don't have to be in love with the idea, but you do have to accept that she is you and vice versa. It's dangerous not to."

"I don't have to accept shit. I will get rid of Koni, even if it means I have to get rid of myself too."

Fuck. Fuck. Fuck.

"Koni?", she questions.

"What?", I respond, trying to come up with any excuse. I draw a complete blank.

"You said get rid of Koni.", she says in a questioning tone while looking up from her notepad. 'You also answered when I asked why you felt a way about Koni stealing your last minute. Another note for when you're pretending, Koni always says Rocky. I assume her full name is Raquel. You may pass with others, but I see you."

"I meant...,' I pause, trying to think of the best comeback. I know there is none, she's been staring at me as if she knew for the last ten minutes. 'Yes, I meant fucking Koni. I don't know why she comes to these sessions; all this shit is useless. I'd never pay anyone to talk about things they know nothing about."

"I finally get to meet you. Why today? Are you thinking about getting rid of you and Koni?" she scribbles something down while maintaining eye contact with me.

"To be honest? I'm sick of Koni trying to get rid of me. She's fucking up my life. I didn't try to mess up hers, so I don't understand why she is putting so much into trying to keep me away. Like you said, I am not going anywhere. I need her to accept that. And for the last time, no, I would not kill us for real."

"But it sounds like you have the same intentions as she does now - to rid yourselves of one another? It will not help either of you."

"I came to protect her because she does a shitty job at it. It's baffling that she finally gets some will about herself just to use it against me. The person that has kept her from tolerating so much bullshit. She's ungrateful, and since she has made it obvious that we both cannot co-exist under her lead, she has to go or take a seat in the background at the very least."

"How have you protected her? What's your first memory, if you don't mind me asking," her pen lets up for the first time in minutes.

"I've protected her in so many ways. She has always been so passive; she let people get away with too much. I came to make sure they could never take anything else from us."

"What did she allow to be taken?", she asks, as if the story is getting good to her. I know this has to be entertaining.

"Everything. The first time I rescued her to save both of us. He was abusive in every way; mentally, emotionally, verbally and physically–every single way. She allowed every bit of it. He turned her into a voluntary victim. She loved him more than she loved us. The first time I came out based on my anger. He and Koni were drinking beers and each had a can in their hand. He had just finished yelling how he had only gotten with her to use her, how he wouldn't have ever considered her if he weren't homeless and topped it off by spitting directly in her face. As soon as he spit, I switched with her immediately. I took the can in my hand and smashed it into his face repeatedly. I was already annoyed by his words, but the spitting? I couldn't contain myself. It was my warning to him that I was done taking his disrespect. You'd have thought he'd learn from that incident, but he didn't."

"He didn't? It takes some people more to learn. Please continue," she says as she scribbles more in her notebook. I continue.

" A couple of months later, he brought a woman in the apartment she was paying for. She came home and caught the girl leaving. When she asked about it, he said she was a crackhead that was trying to find shelter, and he was giving her food to help her out. He slapped her for even questioning him. She weakly apologized. With every action, I grew more furious. He ordered her to stop crying, and as she was trying to stop the tears, he kicked her, she fell to the floor. He got on the floor and started to unbuckle his pants while ripping her shorts off. He grabbed her and told her that she would never deserve better and that he would always treat her like the piece of meat that she is. I screamed for him to back the fuck up. He slapped her hard. I repeatedly screamed at the top of my lungs 'Rape,'" pausing to try to get the pain out of my system. Tears roll down my eyes. Dr.

Rainey passes me a box of Kleenex. I dry my eyes, clear my voice and continue.

'He got pissed and put one hand over her face and his other around her neck. That was my last time sitting back, taking anything from anyone else. I kicked him as hard as I could to get him away from me. He let go, and I watched as his body curled over. He started to reach for his dick; my aim was spot on. I got up, grabbed a knife and warned him not to come any closer. He wouldn't listen. I kept telling him that I would kill him. He didn't listen. I had to take care of it. It was so sick how she became so desperate for his love. He convinced her she wasn't shit when it was him that wasn't. I couldn't stop. I had to make sure that he would never be a problem for us or anyone else. I saved us, and I've been saving our ass from any threat ever since."

“It's important that you remember it's easy to fall victim in extreme situations such as hers. It's much harder to get out of it for most people. Are you only here to protect her? Koni mentioned the trauma caused by him in previous sessions, but she never told me, what happened to Jaylen?”

"Yes, and I'm not stupid. Do you think I would tell you anymore? I've already given you too much. Now you see why I think she's ungrateful. I'm always in charge of saving us. She should be happy that I came when I did, or we'd both be dead by now."

“Well, where is she now? Taking a seat in the background?” Dr. Rainey questions.

“Exactly where she deserves to be. Since that very first incident, I've always had more control than her. I believe I feel things deeper than she ever could. I'm affected differently. She didn't even know I existed until that night at the bar."

"She is stronger than you give her credit for. Like I've told her many times, you will never get her to go away fully. Your goal should be to co-exist, as you have for the past few years?" she questions. I know she's trying to get down to how long I've been around so she can report back to Koni.

"I was fine with that until she wasn't."

"Tell me how you think you are going to get rid of her? It seems like you have the control, so why didn't you take control that very moment that you felt Koni was doing a terrible job in the role?"

"I wanted her to be better. Despite my current actions, I know Koni is our foundation. I know she holds so much shit together. She's mature, and we need someone who knows how to back down, how to remain calm, and someone friendly for networking. I know that Koni has been necessary."

"Ok, if you know she is necessary, why would you try to get rid of her now?"

"Now, I believe I have the necessary skill from sitting back, observing and feeling her. I can fake it until I make it."

"Will I see you while you are 'faking it' or should I say goodbye?"

"Believe it or not doc, you've helped me suppress her. You've allowed the roles to change, just when I thought talk therapy was useless. Without you, we wouldn't be here. I will continue to come in place of Koni as long as it is allowed."

“Our hour is up, but I’d like to extend it. I don’t know if this is my last time getting to have such an open conversation with you.”

"Last time? You must've not been listening. I will see you next week.", I get up and head towards the door. Dr. Rainey stays seated and begins to scribble in her notebook again before I head out the door. That went as well as it could go. Oddly, I do feel better. That session helped me unload things that I've never been able to say to anyone else. It feels good to be able to live my truth out loud.

When I get back home, I see a large white zip-up bag hanging on my front door. It must be the dress Tia had sent over for tonight. I unlock the door and grab the dress on my way inside. I unzip it as soon as I get the door closed. To my surprise, there are two dresses in the bag. One is a floor-length red strapless sweetheart cut dress with a thigh-high split. The bottom is covered in gold beaded embroidery. The second option is a beautiful floor-length sequined black dress. It is one sleeved with a geometric cutout at the bust of the dress and has a silver sequined tail.

Both are gorgeous dresses; I opt for the black because it fits my style a little more. I get the urge to call Tia to thank her for the beautiful options. I know she hand-picked them both, we don't wear the same size, so there is no way that these are her extras. I'm excited to see how gorgeous this dress will look once I get it on. I take a quick shower and start on my hair and makeup. I straighten my hair and pin it up at the back to avoid possible frizz. It'll save me from looking crazy before the event ends. I do myself black smoky eyes, medium lashes, no foundation and clear gloss on my lips. This dress is a statement piece all on its own, no need to overdo it. I finally slide into the dress, and it's a perfect fit.

I have never looked this good; there's something about a fancy-ass dress that will have you feeling untouchable. I wish Gabe could see how beautiful it looks. I take pictures on Koni's phone. With the event being so ritzy, I'd imagine I'll be in at least one photo before the end of the night. Tonight, I don't care too much about pretending to be Koni. I only have to pretend just long enough to get to the event.

She didn't give me too many details; I hope it isn't too boring. Either way, I plan to liven it up a bit. Tia sends a text saying she is downstairs. I put on my sequined silver mules and head out the door. The limo outside waiting caught me off guard. As I walk towards it; the chauffeur opens the door to let me in, I get in and see Tia. She looks damn good. She is wearing a breath-taking powder pink cinched waist sleeveless dress that layers and puffs out at the bottom. Her glitter pink eyelids, dramatic eyelashes and exaggerated cat-eye make her bold eyes pop. Her highlight is blinding.

“Oh, we fancy tonight. Real fancy,” I put both of my pinkies up. Tia starts to laugh.

"Oh, girl. I was just as surprised as you by all of this. He didn't tell me too much about the event, but I can get used to this treatment."

“Speaking of, where is Darius? I thought he'd be at the event too?”

"Oh, he is. He had to be there early to make sure the guest list and venue were set properly. I guess he's worried about what his clients will think. Thank you for coming with me. I couldn't imagine not having someone to talk to all night."

“Thank you for inviting me. This night should be interesting.”

“Interesting?’ she questions as her brow raises. “You know something I don’t?”

“I mean interesting to see how the snobs kick it,” I laugh; she begins to laugh with me.

“We’ll probably be the most down to earth people in the building, besides Darius. Oh, before I forget,” she pulls a bag from the limo floor and brings out two THC pens and a bottle of Crown Vanilla. “You surely didn't think we were going to go in this thing sober. I bought you a pen too; it seems like you'll need it more,” she says as she is handing me a red and gold glittery pen.

I’m genuinely excited about this gift. Although it is meant for Koni, I will get so much use out of it. It’s already loaded with oil; I immediately test it out. I begin to cough after the first inhale, it’s some good shit.

“It’s pretty good, isn’t it? I thought you’d pick the red dress, so I picked a pen that matched,” she says as she hands me a shot of Crown.

“It’s good as fuck. I may need a few backup cartridges before you go. Thank you so much, you were right, I do need it more now.” We take our shots, and she immediately pours another.

“I figured you’d need it fucking around with Ryan. Speaking of, how was therapy? Did you go?”

"Yes, I went. It helped me get through my thoughts today. And Ryan is doing perfectly fine. Let's not talk about any of that depressing shit tonight, ok?" I say to get her to drop any further conversations about it.

"Ok, you're right. Let's enjoy this night. Even if it turns out boring, we'll be sure to get enough pictures in these dresses to last us a decade. New profile picture coming soon," she says and snaps a selfie.

We finally arrive at the event. It's in the dancehall of the State Capitol. The stairs are lit up. There aren't too many visible people outside, but the handful that we do see are dressed to the tee. We get escorted by our chauffeur into the building. Darius is standing at the entrance waiting for us. He is wearing a well-tailored navy suit with a pink pocket square that matches Tia's dress. His shoes are cream, as well as his accent turtleneck. He has a thick gold herringbone necklace on, which pulls the look together. He is sexy as hell, and his cadence shows it too. He looks like a damn model. He stares at Tia and smiles as he grabs her waist and brings her in close.

"Baby, you look so beautiful. Thank you for accompanying me tonight," he looks over at me, "This must be Koni? Tia always speaks so highly of you. It's good to put a face with the name finally. He lets go of Tia and picks my hand up and lightly shakes.

"She talks about you too much; I can't get her to shut up sometimes." I half-smile and force a giggle. "It's good to meet you. Thank you for having me at such a beautiful event."

"Oh, you haven't seen anything yet ladies. Let's go inside," he says as he takes Tia's hand and leads us to the ballroom.

"I have to go check on something ladies, I'll get back with you all in a few," he kisses Tia and walks into the crowd. I'd guess there are around one hundred guests. The room is full of beautiful dresses and nice suits. Tia begins to point out some of her other clients that were in attendance. I begin to scan the room. The room is dripping in gold and white décor. Everything is beautiful. There's a large stage in the middle of the room. Servers are walking around wearing slacks and button-downs with hors d'oeuvre and drink trays. They even have two huge ice sculptures, one in the shape of a T; the other is a D; both in cursive. This is some fancy-ass shit; I love every detail. I hear Tia mumble something to herself. She looks confused. She repeats herself but louder.

"Is that my mom?"

"Huh?"

"Girl, my mom. Did you see her? I thought I just did, but now I don't see her anymore", she says scanning the crowd.

I begin to look in the direction she is looking in just as Darius comes over a microphone.

"Tia, please come join me on stage beautiful," the microphone echoes through the room. The crowd begins to quiet down.

"I'll be back," she says to me as she turns away and begins to walk toward the stage. I look up on the stage and see him standing there now with the mic in his hand. His voice matches everything about him. She gets to the stage, he helps her up and takes her hand with one hand, a mic in the other. He leans in and kisses her, then turns back to the crowd.

"Thank you all for coming here. It's going to be a beautiful event with beautiful people. None of us would be here if it weren't for my baby," he turns to Tia, "tonight we honor you." He bows. Tia giggles.

"Honor me? Baby what?' she asks and looks to the crowd. Her parents are waving. She begins waving back and looking confused. Her eyes begin to gloss over 'Wait? You did all of this for me?"

"Yes. Since I've known you, you've worked your ass off. You have always excelled in everything you've touched, and you are the definition of a self-made boss. Not only are you beautiful and smart, you're crazy sexy too,' he glances over to the crowd. 'But only I can say that. We've been low key, but I know you have to be feeling this the same as me. I go after what I want, and you are one I never want to let go. If it's too soon, please tell me," he gets down on one knee and pulls out a black box, "Tia Walton, will you marry me?" he says looking up at her through glossy eyes.

"Yes! Yes! Yes! Baby! Look at this ring!! Put it on, put it on," she screams with excitement and begins to wave her hand impatiently.

He takes the ring out and slides it on her finger. She pulls him up from the floor and jumps into his arms.

"It's so pretty. All of this is so beautiful. This is perfect. I love you so much!" She leans in and kisses him.

A fucking engagement. How am I supposed to be a

bitch at a fucking engagement? I hit the THC pen again and settle on having a good time since I'm here anyway. Xay is coming over tonight, and I want to be feeling myself before I go home. Tia comes back over, holding out her hand to show off her ring. It's breath-taking. It must be at least 6 carats, princess cut, with a white gold band. It fits her perfectly.

"Bitchhh, can you believe this? Look at this ring! I didn't know he was going to propose, bitch, I'm engaged!" she sticks her hand out and begins wiggling her fingers.

"He did a great job picking out the ring. Congratulations." I try to fake enthusiasm.

"Damn. That was dry as fuck. Girl look at his fine ass! He's so good to me, and he's rich!! We've talked about this since the first time I stalked him on Twitter. What's up with you?"

"Nothing. I am happy for you," trying to sound more enthused this time. She begins to stare me down.

"You're not Koni, are you? Fuck, I should've peeped this with your dry ass on the phone. She would be so mad that I couldn't tell immediately." She shakes her head as she rolls her eyes.

"I'm good at being Koni if I do say so myself. I came to fuck with you but decided against it with him proposing and all. I don't care, but I know how bad you wanted this, so my Congratulations was at least sincere. Please be happy that I'm deciding to chill."

"Oh girl, if you tried some stupid shit tonight, I'd be on your ass. You wouldn't ruin this for me. What is your deal anyway? How can you come and go, but Koni can't? Where is Koni?"

"She's obviously not here, so what does it matter. I spared you; you aren't as annoying as I originally thought. If you're cool, I'm cool, and we're cool moving forward."

"Is Koni coming back? I'd much rather share this moment with her than you, no offense."

"None taken. If I knew this was going to be an engagement party, I would've declined the invitation anyway. And the verdict is still out on Koni. I'd suggest you worry about yourself tonight and enjoy your man. I will Uber back home."

"No, don't leave. You're a complete bitch, but I am still glad to have the presence of my best friend here. I don't care what your name is tonight; you are my best friend. We are going to turn up and worry about this other shit later. I know that you at least know how to party."

"Are you sure? I don't want your people thinking I am doing the most because I'm not basic like Koni."

"Watch it. Yes, I am sure. Whatever you do tonight, I'll just say you were wasted, so let's drink up bitch," she flags a server down and grabs two glasses of wine from the tray. "It's nice to finally meet you, Congra-tu-mother-fucking-lations to my damn self," she raises her glass, and I raise mine and clink it with hers.

"Congra-tu-fucking-lations to you, bestie! I am so happy for you," the words coming out like vomit. Forced and unwanted, but there is no indication of that in the tone. I didn't say those words. It must be Koni. But how?

"That's more like it!" she grabs two more glasses of wine as a server passes by. "We have so much planning to do, all three of us!"

Chapter 10

I feel a kiss on my forehead that wakes me out of my sleep. My head is resting on Xay's chest, with his arms wrapped tight around me. After getting home from Tia's engagement party, Xay was already here waiting for me. He had a hot bath run with a trail of pink roses leading to my bedroom. It was lit up with candles, and there was light music playing softly in the background. Up until last night, we had still been fucking in Koni's bed. It all caught me by surprise.

When I got in, I was wasted and expecting nasty drunk sex. Last night, however, we made love for the first time. He was the perfect gentleman. He bathed me, dried me off, oiled me down and carried me to the bed. I've never had anyone put so much effort into setting the mood. The sex was better than anything I ever had. He kissed my body from head to toe. He ate my pussy slow and delicate, I don't know if it was because of the drugs or liquor, but the sex brought me to tears. I always thought that sweet shit was for boring people who didn't know how to really fuck, but last night I found out differently.

"Good morning, beautiful. How'd you sleep?"

"Amazing. Last night was amazing. I've never felt anything like it."

"I can tell. You came fourteen times. Yes, I counted. Koni has never done that, and neither have you since you've been here. I wanted to do something special for you."

"I know; you almost broke me. My body couldn't handle all the feelings I felt; I couldn't stop cumming. Even when you stopped touching me, I don't know what that was, but I loved every bit of it."

"I mind fucked you. I knew you'd like it, even with you playing the hard-ass you are,' he chuckles, looks down at me, and kisses me on the lips. 'I enjoyed every bit of you too. I hope I don't lose you anytime soon. Can you keep a secret?"

"You won't. I used to take over for Koni before you met me at random times. I just tried steering clear of the relationship to be respectful. I only came out to talk to you when I needed something new. Koni doesn't like half the shit in here." I move one arm out in a swooping motion across the room. "You took care of me, even before you really knew me. I hope I never lose you." I lean in and flick my tongue slowly over his lips. "And with all of my secrets that you know? Spill it." I lay back on his chest.

"That explains why Koni acted like she didn't practically beg me for these walls. Technically, she didn't. It was you. Sneaky, sneaky. Don't tell…," he pauses and begins to smile. "…yourself, but it's like you read my mind sexually. I thought Koni was the best I had, until you. She only refused to do a few things, and I was cool with that. But you're so open. This still blows my mind. I wish you came sooner."

"I thought you loved Koni? It sounds like you want me around for good?" I raise off his chest to look in his eyes.

"I do love Koni. But I wouldn't be terribly disappointed to have two girlfriends, what man would," he laughs as he keeps eye contact.

“Two? What if I was the only one?” I roll my eyes.

“Koni isn’t coming back? Ever? What happened to your boyfriend, Gavin? George? Or whatever his name is?”

"Gabe. I'm sure you know exactly what his name is. He's away right now and maybe permanently. Right along with Koni." I wait for his expression to show me who his head really lies with.

“So Koni isn’t coming back? I feel crazy saying this and looking at your face. I’m still not fully used to it.” I can’t tell if he’s happy or sad, he looks more confused than anything. I feel his body begin to tense up. He probably doesn’t know what he feels himself.

"She may not. You didn't answer my question. I have a weird feeling with you; I need to know if it's something worth exploring or if I'm just fun for you to fuck while your main chicks away. I don't think Koni likes this. You’re hers technically, but I can't help but want you too. It makes more sense for us to have the same man." I begin to rub his back as I slowly plant kisses on his face. I never thought that finding someone we both liked would be possible based on our taste being so different. Xay is universal; we need that.

“I tried showing you last night. You are more than just sex to me. I don’t want to get too wrapped up in this conversation until I know what’s what,” he pulls away from my kisses.

"Oh, you don't want to hurt her feelings, huh?" I ask, rolling my neck to let him know to tread lightly.

I see his lips move, but I can no longer hear him. I hear a faint voice whispering.

"Xay! I'll be back. Don't fall for her. I love you. Xay! Xay?" the distorted voice fades in.

Since last night, the voice keeps playing in my head. I'm either losing my mind, or its Koni unsuccessfully trying to regain control. It doesn't sound like her. The voice is muffled, so, to be fair, it doesn't sound like anyone. It's not that easy to switch, but I'm mad that she's trying. I'm mad that I can hear her at all.

"Hello? Anyone there?" Xay asks, pulling me from my thoughts. He's waving his hand in my face to try to get my attention.

"Where else would I be Xay? I got lost in thought, that's all." I say casually to deflect.

"Hell if I know. You were just staring. Your eyes looked empty. Are you ok?" he questions, with concern displayed across his expression.

"Yes, I'm good. I have to start getting ready for work; we'll continue this conversation later." I lean in to kiss him, get out of bed, and start getting ready for today.

I feel bad that I can't be with Gabe. He still hasn't contacted me since being out. I've tried calling a few more times since Raquel told me he was out. Xay asking about Gabe has me evaluating my feelings for them both. I thought Gabe was perfect for me before now. I think I'm falling in love with Xay. He accepts me. So does Gabe, but Xay loves us both. I'm not opposed to sharing him if Koni comes back; neither am I about Tia. Last night showed me a different side of her. She's nowhere near as prude as Koni.

We both got so fucked up and were the life of the party. Even if it was just the liquor and weed, she didn't treat me any differently once she figured out I wasn't her best friend. She made me feel welcome and not like something was wrong with me. She talked to me as my own person; she asked me to stay even though I had ill intentions for her by attending, to begin with. She even called me Ryan, the entire night. None of it mattered to her. For that, she gets to stay.

I glance over at Xay, who is still lying in the bed. He's been watching me the entire time I've been getting ready. He must be off today. I bend over in a wide-legged stance before I slide my skirt on, look back to make sure he's still watching and start to rub my pussy slowly. I rub until each finger is coated in pre cum. I walk over to him and spread my fingers across his face.

"Something to keep this pussy on your mind all day. A little more than usual,' I pause to stick my middle finger in my mouth and suck it slowly while staring in his eyes. 'Mmm, you can taste the pineapples today," I say as I repeat it with the other fingers. He licks his lips and I watch as he scoops some off the side of his face and put it in his mouth.

"You will always be my favorite snack, "he says with the sexiest smirk on his face.

"Boy, I'm a whole damn meal. I'm everyone's favorite," I add jokingly.

I pull my skirt up, slide into my loafers and begin to gather the things I will need today. Although he isn't technically my man, it feels so good to feel normal for a change. I walk over and kiss him on my way out the door and head to the office. Shelly is sitting at her desk when I arrive with a huge bouquet of pink tulips. They're beautiful.

"Oh, girl, who sent these?" I say as I pick one up and put it under my nose. She swats my hand and takes it back.

"These are mine today, boss lady! Let me bask in it because there's a first for everything. Gabriel's fine ass sent them. It's something about that old man that drives me crazy," she picks up one and inhales deep like she usually does with Koni's.

"Probably that good dick. I haven't had it or anything, but girl, you can tell how that man walks that he's blessed." Her eyes widen, and she places her hand over her mouth as she gasps.

"Girl, I have never heard you speak like that, and I don't kiss and tell," she leans in and whispers, "But blessed indeed. He don't even need that blue pill girl." We both begin to laugh.

"Ok! Look who has the juice now. Owww."

"Koni! You did not just owww, girl, what has gotten into you? I've been working for you for two years and this is the most open you've been. I love this new you."

"You are? Well great! I'm trying to show more of my true self these days. Koni can be so boring sometimes."

"Oh, let me find out you got an alter ego? What's this

egos name?"

"I'm thinking something cute and simple, like Ryan."

"Ryan? Nah. This new you is more of a Candi. Can be sweet, spicy, but she's sexy either way," she laughs. Her phone begins to ring. She picks it up,

"It's a great day at Given Investments. You've reached the desk of Koni Reese, what can I assist you with today?" she recites in her professional voice. I hear mumbling through the phone. Her face begins to scrunch up.

"Gabe? Calm down. I don't know what you're saying. Do you want to speak to Koni or no?" I hear more mumbling.

"Girl here. I can't make out a word he's saying. I think I'm tripping because I swore I just heard him call you Ryan. Unless?' she raises her eyebrow, 'Is Ryan your freak name? You better not be cheating on Xay ass," she continues to stare at me. I take the phone from her and wave my hand in a dismissive motion. I walk into my office and close the door to finish the conversation.

"Hello?"

"Ry, I know that's you, baby. Rocky told me you were back. That bitch Koni is trying to ruin my life. We have to get rid of her sooner than later."

"What? Gabe, how is that even possible? She didn't know you until recently and still doesn't know anything but what you've told her about you."

"Nah. She's up to something. She doesn't want us to be

happy. This shit came out of nowhere; I don't fuck with anyone but you, Rocky and my dad. It had to be her. Or him. He ain't shit, so I really wouldn't put it past him either."

"What? Why would either of them try to hurt you, Gabe?"

"Baby, you just have to trust me on this. I don't want to discuss this on the phone. Can I meet up with you sometime this weekend? Maybe tomorrow?"

"Well, I missed you and it's been me trying to contact you the whole time, you could've answered once just to see. But yea, that's cool. You can come by my place, or I'll meet you at yours."

"The police have been all through my shit. I think it'd be best to meet at yours. What time are you thinking?"

"I'm free all day. I'll be there all day, so just call me to let me know you're on the way."

"Ok baby. And please, don't tell anyone about this. I don't know who to trust right now. I'll see you soon."

"I won't. See you tomorrow." I hang up the phone.

Rocky was right. Something is off about him but I'm happy he finally reached out. I was beginning to worry that he never would. I typically tune out during Koni's workdays, so I'm not sure how her meetings typically go with Gabriel or any of her other clients. I doubt that Koni has anything to do with it, though. More than likely, it's his father. All the shit he's told me about that man, I wouldn't put anything past him. He's so selfish; he'd do anything to save his ass. I hear a knock at the door, before I can respond, Shelly walks through the door.

"So, is this alter ego sleeping with Gabe or nah? Because honey, something has gotten into you. If it's Gabe, I want all the tea," she smirks.

"Girl, no. I was just playing about the Ryan thing. He was calling for business for his father. Nothing more, nothing less. Come on now, do I seem like the type to cheat?" I almost laugh at myself for playing so much.

"This last week? You do," she laughs.

"I wouldn't. I take my relationships seriously, so no tea today. Besides, I'm sure with you having a thing with his father; you'd surely know if I decided to creep."

"To be honest, I don't think they have that great of a relationship. I tried asking about him, and he didn't give me too much info on him. I was trying to set him up with my homegirl."

"He's taken," I pause. "Or at least I think he is. He mentioned something about a girlfriend in the last meeting I had with him."

"Damn. Of course, he is, all the fine ones usually are. I'm surprised someone hasn't snatched his dad up by now. But I'm glad they didn't because I'm pulling out every trick for this man. He won't be going anywhere anytime soon."

"Tricks only go so far. You get a better deal when you keep it real, ever heard the saying?"

"I'm surprised you've heard the saying and even more surprised you just used it," she laughs. "I gotta get used to this new you shit. But please believe, I got this one wrapped around my finger."

"Bloop. Let me mind my own business then."

"Bloop? Girl, who have you been hanging around? Whoever it is, make sure you keep them. I love this. Let me get back to work." She walks back into the lobby and closes her door on the way out. Everyone in Koni's life is adapting well to me; this is much easier than I thought it would be.

It's almost been one full week of being Koni, and I think I'm doing a much better job than she ever did. This newfound freedom is amazing. I never knew what it meant to be myself until now. I'm finding out things that I like as well as getting to explore things that Koni never did by being cooped up in the house all the time. In the last week, I've attended an art show, an open mic poetry night and even went to a fancy wine tasting event with Tia. She's worried about Koni and when she'll return, but that doesn't stop her from communicating with me just as much.

I've gained a friend, while possibly losing another, Raquel. I miss her so much. I've been calling her all week and finally got her to agree to meet up with me tonight. She has been my ride or die since my first night out; I can't get her out of my head. I need the opportunity to give her the apology she deserves, and if she won't have me as her lover, I will settle for just her friendship.

I hear a knock on my door; I assume it's Shelly, I wait for her to invite herself in as usual. She doesn't. I hear another knock.

"Yes, please come in," I say, annoyed.

The door opens, and its Gabriel. Koni doesn't have him on the list of clients for today, so this is random.

"Hey, Koni. Sorry to drop in on you. I came by to bring Shelly some lunch but wanted to know if you had a moment to go over a few things?"

"Sure, I'm free for the next hour or so. Please come in and have a seat," I wave my hand in a welcoming motion.

He walks in and closes the door behind him. He begins fidgeting with his watch, I have no choice but to notice it's the same watch I've been eyeballing for myself recently, but in the men's style - A gorgeous yet simple Interlocking G Gucci watch. He's wearing black slacks, a black short sleeve button down that's opened a little at the top to show his neat chest hair. He looks just as good as he usually does.

"I can't stay too long. I just wanted to let you know that all my clients have agreed to the transfer over. We can meet up later next week to sign everything over in your name if that works for you?"

"Oh, that's great news. Next week works fine for me. How's next Wednesday at 2 pm?"

"Perfect. I'll have all their finance information sent over to you sometime this weekend. Please keep it to yourself. I don't want Shelly to know the specifics of what's going on. Or anyone else for that matter," he says, lowering his tone.

"No worries. Everything is just between you and me," I assure.

"I know I can trust you. Also," he pauses and begins to whisper, "Good looking out on the situation with my son. I won't have to do any time now. I knew they were watching. I can't thank you enough for getting them off my back. I'm too old to go back there. He's young; he'll get through it, just like I did when I was around his age."

I sit in silence and stare at him with a blank expression. He continues.

"I know it may be hard now; you may be missing him. But you told me that you wanted him out of your life, for good. Just know that he won't be able to bother you for a few years at minimum once he is sentenced. There's nothing he can do to get out of it."

My eyes begin to water. I don't know how this happened. Gabe isn't just tripping like I thought he was. Koni did set him up. All of this to get him out of her life, which also gets him out of mine. If I could kill the bitch, I would. He walks over to me and places his hand on my back.

"Don't cry. The time will go by quickly for him. And its Fed time, so it isn't as bad as it sounds. I know you must think I am a terrible person, but we're the same. Sometimes sacrifices must be made. How do you think I've remained so wealthy?"

"You're right. It's different now that it's too late to take it all back.' I lie to stay in character. I begin to wipe the tears from my face. "But I know this is for the best. For you and me."

"It is for the best. I won't tell if you won't."

"I'm the best secret keeper you'll ever meet in your life. Wednesday will be the start of your greatness."

"You've shown me, and I trust that you'll continue to be. It's time to boss up. See you soon, boss lady." He closes the door as he walks out.

I originally wanted this deal to advance and use it to travel and be away from everyone in Koni's life. I thought it was my way out. Now that I have taken over, I no longer need an out. I can't imagine doing business with a man that is comfortable with his flesh and blood, taking the fall for his dirt. Together he and Koni have managed to do away with the love of my life, both for selfish reasons. I wouldn't even believe Koni could do something this terrible. She finally knows how to protect herself, too bad she chose the wrong person to fuck over. She can't fuck me without getting fucked. As the saying goes, 'Hell has no fury like a woman scorned.' Both of them will pay for this; I'll have the last and best laugh.

Chapter 11

I open the door to see Raquel standing outside in a long sheer jacket with a red lace bodysuit underneath; it doesn't leave much to the imagination. The lace is cut out into a bralette and thong with elastic straps going across her belly to connect the two pieces. Her titties are sitting perfectly. She strides in the door with her thigh-high black latex boots on, gripping a whip with tassels in her hand. I close the door behind her. She looks so fucking sexy.

"Well, hello there. I thought you said we weren't doing this anymore," I say, my eyes scanning her from head to toe.

"Oh, shut up and just fuck me, will you?"

"Raquel, this isn't what I called you over here for. I owe you a sincere apology."

"You do. But it can wait. I said I want to be fucked. When have you ever had a problem with that? You better not be nice either."

She walks over to me and starts to pull my over-sized T-shirt over my head. She slides my leggings off next. I made sure to wear something casual this time because I didn't want her to feel like I was trying to disrespect her in any way. I'm left in only my black silk thong. She doesn't have to tell me again; I've been craving her pussy. It's been too long. I pull her jacket off and hang it at the door. I walk over to the couch, and she follows. I stop, turn around and snatch the whip out of her hand.

"Stop right there. I want you to crawl to me. You look so sexy. Get down on your knees and crawl to me, now." I walk over to the couch and sit on the edge.

"How'd you know I brought that for you to use?" she asks sexily.

She gets down on her knees and crawls over towards me slowly. I'm wet at the sight of her being so obedient. She knows that I'm a control freak—she loves it. Once she reaches me, I smack her on the ass with the whip hard. She moans loud and sits up on her knees.

"Get naked. This is sexy as hell,' I comment, reaching out and flicking the top of her bodysuit, "but you know I love looking at your body. Keep the boots on."

She gets up and slowly slides the lace off her shoulders. She starts to dance as she slides it down her hips and lets it drop to the floor. She gets back in position, on her knees in front of me. I pull her up on the couch as I slide down to the floor to switch places with her. I open her legs wide and begin to lick her pussy. She's dripping wet already. I slurp to taste her juices and then begin to lick her clit. She begins to squirm around the couch. I tap her on the ass and pin both of her legs back in the air as I lick it faster. I slurp on it while rubbing my face in her juices. She is moaning so loud. I lift from her pussy and look up at her. Her eyes are closed, and head tilted back. She opens her eyes and looks down at me.

"Cum in my mouth. Do it nasty." I don't give her time to respond before I go back to licking her clit. She pulls back and places her hand on my chin. She pulls my face up and meets me with a kiss me. She kisses in a way to be sure to lick all of her juices off my face. She's not ready to cum yet; I can tell she's trying to hold back. I get up off the floor, grab her hand, and pull her off the couch. We go to my bedroom. I push her on the bed and begin to straddle her face backward. I feel her tongue flick over my clit as I begin to lean forward and spread her legs, using her boots as leverage. I bury my face in her pussy and get in a comfortable position so she can eat mine like I like too. We both begin moaning. I grind on her face and stick my finger in her ass while continuing to eat her pussy. She loses it.

"Yea, eat my pussy like that. Nasty just like that." I say as I grind harder on her face.

She cums all over my face. I don't stop. Her legs close in on my face as she squirts. I get up, turn my body around and start to suck on her perfect gumdrop sized hard nipple while fondling the other in my hand. She starts rubbing my pussy with one hand and playing with my nipples with the other. Her nipples are so perfect; I cum hard just feeling it in my mouth. I cum all over her hand. She pulls her hand away and licks it slowly. She reaches over and puts two fingers in my mouth to taste; I happily lick it up. We kiss each other and lay back on the bed in bliss.

"I'll miss this Ry," she sits up and begins to run her hands through my hair.

"Miss? Why? Where are you going?" I lift up too.

"Nowhere. I meant what I said last time, and girl, what a hell of a way to go out. I just needed to get this last one in. I can't have the inconsistency in a lover. But I can be your best friend still," she says, still rubbing my hair. I thought this meant we were back to our regularly scheduled program, but she really came on some player shit.

"Ok. I can feel that. I'm going to miss fucking on you, but I felt I needed to apologize to save the friendship, not the sex. I didn't mean to rub you wrong by coming off that way either. You're right, I should've contacted you sooner, and I have no real excuse as to why I didn't. I felt that you'd automatically understand, so communication wasn't necessary, and I was wrong. I'm sorry."

"I did understand, but then my feelings were involved. It's just time for me to take them out. I don't know how long you'll even know my name, so I can't do that to myself again." She stops rubbing my hair and turns her back toward me as she shifts to the end of the bed.

"I'll know it forever, but I get what you're saying. I'm just thankful for our new relationship moving forward."

My face scrunches as I watch her get out of the bed and begin to get dressed.

"You can chill for a minute! There is no rush. Damn, you must be headed to the next bitch's house?" I question, sliding to the edge of the bed, standing up and searching the room for a top.

"No need to prolong it either. Can we do some regular

friend shit next week? Maybe lunch? Or dinner. Since the bar has been closed down, I've been completely free." She continues to get dressed.

"It's still shut down? Are you still getting paid, at least?" I begin walking towards her as I slide my arms into my fuzzy white robe.

"Oh, yea. Gabriel gave me a nice chunk of change for discretion regarding other things that happen in the bar if ever asked. I'm set for as long as it takes to re-open. I'm good." she lifts her hands toward the ceiling in praise.

"I always knew it was shady shit going on in that bar." I begin to recall all of the weird shit I've seen in there the last couple of years.

"Girl, you don't know the half. Well, I don't know what you know. But I'm sure you're smart enough to at least peep the drugs. Gabriel only opened that damn bar so he could maintain his status in the drug game. But really, that drug shit is nothing compared to the fuckery he's really involved in," she bows her head and begins to shake it. "You know why those girls come in there dressed the way they do? They're house girls," she pauses and begins to nod her head in a yes motion. I'm guessing in response to my facial expression. "Yes, house girls! Most of them are over 18. I'm only telling you because Gabe is facing more than just laundering charges. It's serious shit," she looks sad for him.

I know they've been good friends for a while now, so she's losing her only other friend aside from me. She takes a seat toward the edge of my bed, on my cream plush bench, I follow and sit next to her.

"Damn. What? This is crazy. Did Gabe know about all

this shit? I don't understand why it's only falling on him and not his father. It's his club."

"Gabe only knew about the drugs, nothing else. His dad thought he wouldn't be down if he knew about any of the other shit. I get paid well, and it's mostly because I know about it all. Gabriel isn't stupid by far. I'd never snitch, even without the extra money because that's just not my thing. Sadly, he's going down for this shit by himself, though. I really fucked with Gabe."

"I did too. You know how happy he makes me. I'm heartbroken, honestly. He finally contacted me; I'm going to meet with him later tonight. Even though I don't want to accept it, I know I need to prepare to say goodbye," my eyes begin to water. She puts her arm around me and hugs me tight.

"It'll be ok, Ry. I'll be here to adjust to life without him for a while. Whoever fucked him over, will pay. My bet's on Gabriel. That shit will come back on him, I believe it," she let's go of her grip and puts her arms back down to her side.

"Thank you for coming by and for the revamp of an even better friendship, "I say, embracing what the future holds. We both stand up and walk over to the door.

"I'll be talking to you soon. I'm so glad you answer the phone now; a few good things have come from this disaster after all." She walks out the door, rocking the hell out of those boots. I close it behind her and head to the restroom.

I turn on the shower and hop in. Xay will be here in about an hour. Raquel has been available to me since we met, but I'm ok with this. It's for the best. Besides, Xay is taking good care of me sexually. I haven't even craved anyone else. Not even Gabe. Raquel has always had a special part of me. I don't mess with women outside of threesomes, but Raquel is special. We vibe on all levels but she deserves more than I can really give her. I'm happy she's still choosing to have me in her life. She's also fully accepting of me. It's so rare to find genuine friends; it'd be foolish of me to let that go.

❁❁❁

"Did she suck on your pussy better than me? Tell me all the details." He walks towards me and begins to kneel.

"I don't know if it was better. You'll have to give me something to compare it to." He slides my panties down and puts his face in my pussy. I begin to tell him every detail of what just happened with Rocky. His dick is rock hard and jumping as I tell him. He's eating my pussy so good. I tell him how she came all over my face, he gets up, flips me around and pushes me against the wall. He slides his dick in me slowly.

"Did she make you cum more than me? Was it better? It won't hurt my feelings, answer my question," he demands, giving my ass a hard smack.

"No. No one makes me cum better than you. No one has ever been close." I can hardly get the words out.

He thrusts in and out while grinding his hips in a circular motion. I can feel him tapping my g-spot. I moan his name as my body begins to vibrate uncontrollably. I cream all over his dick. He slides it out and admires it. He rubs my pussy slowly as I lay back, trying to regroup.

Everything is different with Xay. I talk to him about any and everything. I've openly spoken about fucking Gabe and Raquel. He never judges or shuns me; he is always a listening ear; it also doesn't hurt that he's one of the best dicks I've ever had. This was the first time he requested to hear about me getting off with someone else during sex; the shit turned me on immensely. Having someone completely accept me is extremely sexy. The thought of not having to keep secrets from anyone seems like a dream come true. I know it had to be hard, initially, for him to hear stories from someone who shares the same body as someone he thought was exclusive to him. He's never shown it.

"Can I tell you something? Just you?"

"Xay, you should know you can tell me anything. I tell you all my shit."

"I've always thought Koni was the woman I'd marry. But I had one small issue with her. I've never had a sexual soulmate until you came. I love her, and she's good, but sometimes she's so shy it's like I have to coerce her to fuck me. You though? My God, the connection is unreal. You're on the same shit I'm on, no matter what."

"We do have good sex. But I've always wanted someone who wants me for more than just that. I can get dick and pussy anywhere and believe me–I have. I don't know where your head is. If I stay, it's not a mix of Koni and I. It's just me. You'll be stuck with only me. You seem to have a fantasy, and all I am is the one who came and fulfilled it for you. Which is cool, but don't act like you really want more than just this fire ass pussy," I look directly in his eyes. I want him to take my words seriously.

"No, Ryan. You are so much more than that. You don't

realize how much you are like Koni. It's like someone pulled all her strengths and put them in you. You're an asshole though. She's sweeter than you. But I know, under your hard-ass persona, you can be sweet as well," he says with a straight face, shrugging his shoulders.

My strengths? How fucking dare he. He'll miss my sweet ass if I ever come back. The voice is back. I know it's Koni now, aside from the words, I can now feel her. She feels like she finally shares the anger that I have.

"I wasn't sure if you being here was a fluke or what, but these last couple of weeks with you have confirmed that you are my soulmate in every way. I'm no longer afraid to say it to you, Ryan. I love Koni, but I am fully in love with you," he lifts on his elbows in bed, leans in over me and begins to stare while he gently caresses my face.

You're nothing like me. Men are so stupid thinking with their dicks all the time. Xay, I thought you were different, she hisses. I shake my arms in an attempt to shake the feeling and voice away.

"You love me? You don't even know me," I move his hand from my face.

"But I do. You're honest, and you're open. You've told me everything and let me decide how I want to proceed. Or if I even want to proceed at all. I'm rocking with you. I know I've never had this connection with any other soul, including Koni," he touches my face again, but this time, lifting my chin to him and beginning to kiss all over my face.

Fuck you Xay! she tries to interrupt.

"I know I love you. I've had a lot of feelings I'm not

used to this past week. Probably finally feeling what Koni has been so lucky to get to feel." He slows down with his kisses and stares at me with a smile on his face for a minute in silence.

"So, it's not just me? I don't want to lose you, Ryan. I don't think I'll find anyone like you."

"Let's just focus on now. Strength is important; I've always had it. I'm still learning how to use it, but as long as I can, I'll keep choosing you."

He lays next to me and wraps his arms tightly around me. I tell him about my meeting with Gabe tonight. He agrees to leave as not to cause any conflict. I don't know what I'm going to say to him. I will miss him more than I can express. I can't hold him down, that's not even in consideration. I've never been the type to ride or die, I can't do shit with a nigga in jail. I hate it for him. I'm going to help him in the only way I can think of.

Chapter 12

I hear a car pull into the driveway. I peek out the blinds in my living room and see a white and black challenger. Gabe gets out of the car and heads towards the door. I walk towards the door and open it before he can knock.

"Hey baby!', he picks me up and begins to spin me around while hugging me tightly. He lowers me back down, leans in, kisses me and continues. "It's some crazy shit going on, but it's so good to be able to finally see you again."

"It's good to see you too Gabe. I've been so worried about you ever since that night they took you to jail," my eyes scanning him from head to toe, taking notice of how casually he's dressed. The entire time I've known him, I've never seen him dressed this simple, in his white T-shirt, basketball shorts and white Air Force ones. This would usually be an outfit he talks about other men for wearing. He's so flashy; he usually wouldn't be caught dead in anything that doesn't draw attention.

"I thought you said it wasn't you that night? It was

Koni, right? I thought it was you, but you ...or she told me it wasn't. So, you really were there?" he asks as he walks towards the couch and makes himself comfortable.

"It's complicated, but yes. I was there with Koni. Those were my words. I was heartbroken to see you like that." I sit on the edge of my couch to make him feel more comfortable.

"Baby, it was that bitch that set me up. I don't mean no harm, but that uppity bitch was trying to get rid of me," his veins jumping as he balls his fists and places them down by his sides.

"Why do you think that? Koni is a sweet person Gabe." I scoot closer to him on the couch. I need him to stay calm. His temper gets just as ugly as mine; I know things can quickly escalate out of hand.

"Shit, maybe to you or whoever else she has you fucking! But with me? She has always been dry and has always given me a bad vibe. I only stuck around because I couldn't give up on getting you back." he stands up and begins to pace in circles around my floating glass coffee table.

"You still didn't say why you thought that. It could've just been timing Gabe or someone else." I say calmly, as I get up, walk towards him and lightly place my hand in the center of his back. He stops pacing.

"I don't want this going anywhere other than this room," he says, lowering his voice as he grabs my wrist and applies pressure.

He looks directly in my eyes and nods his head slowly up and down. He continues until I nod my head back in agreeance then drops my wrist; his eyes gaze the room as he continues.

"My dad told me it was her. He said the last time they had a meeting she wanted to take over his business. She was desperate and willing to do anything to get me out of the way," he pauses, studies my face for what I'm assuming is any hint that any of this is familiar to me, and continues.

"She handles all the business accounts and reports now. It seems that she had it out for me. She switched the bar over to my name without me knowing. G had been telling her shit was getting hot, she told him not to worry and that she'd get the heat off of him. Until that last meeting where she mentioned how much she wanted me out of her life, he had no idea she was out for me. He told me he tried to even pay her to keep quiet, and to make sure him and I walked free when he first hired her. She took the money and still snitched, but not on him, only on me!" he yells as he stands up, waving his balled fist in the air.

I can tell he's angry. I've seen him like this several times in the past. I thought I caught a whiff of bourbon when he first hugged me, but I brushed it off until now. His ass has been drinking; there is no reasoning with him right now.

"Gabe, all of this sounds like a bit much. How can you trust what he says? How do you know it wasn't him like you hinted on the phone?" I roll my eyes, unknowingly, before looking back up at him, being mindful to keep a look of concern on my face instead of irritation. It's like defusing a bomb when he goes on his anger-driven drinking binges.

"I ain't speak to him until last night. He told me everything he knew because I confronted him, thinking it was him. He told me everything he knew. Ry, I was going to kill him. I don't think you know how serious this shit really is," his tone is now eerily calm.

"Kill him? Gabe, no! He's your father no matter what. So, what are you here for? To kill me instead?" I ask, my voice raising as I hop off the couch and lean back into my hip.

"Baby, I would never hurt you again. But if I could kill Koni and keep you, I'd take that chance in a heartbeat. I know that's not how shit works. I came here to tell you what's up." He unrolls his fist while he attempts to straighten his face.

"No offense, but I wouldn't trust shit your father says. He's a scumbag. He shouldn't be trusted. I don't know what really happened so I can't speak on it. But I highly doubt it was us. You keep saying Koni did it, but that's ultimately my body. Meaning any consequences would affect me too. How can you be so in love with one of us and hate the other? How do you think that'll ever work out in the long run?"

I feel tears on the verge of surfacing. I fight them. I vowed long ago, never to let him see me weak again.

"Baby, the way this shit is playing out, there won't be a long run for me. It was shit going on in that club that I didn't even know about until they fucking charged me for it. I have a good lawyer, but even he is telling me things aren't looking good. The only way I could even get some of this shit reduced is to snitch on G and I ain't no snitch," he lowers his head and begins to pace the floor again.

"He ain't shit, though. Hell, for all you know, he is the one who has you in this position. He's the one who had you running his bar, right? You only started as a favor to him."

"I started as a favor to myself. He owed me for not being in my life, so when the opportunity came up, I hopped on it. You right though, he ain't shit, but he ain't no snitch either. How do you think he ended up in jail the first time? He could've snitched and gotten off completely. Ain't no bitch in his blood. It was Koni, I know it," his voice gets louder with every word he says.

"You mean it was me," I correct him.

It was me. Good riddance too, she chimes into my thoughts right on cue.

"No baby. I know what you're saying, but you should know what I mean," he fidgets with his hands.

My phone begins to ring. I walk over to my dining table and press the side button to silence it. It's Xay, now is not a good time to talk. Gabe seems like he's in a fragile state, and I don't want anything sending him over the edge.

"Who is that? One of your other niggas?" he questions, glancing over at my phone.

My man, that she stole. I hear Koni correct me in my head.

"Gabe, where is this coming from? You know me! Stop it. It's Xay, and you see that I ignored it because I'm right where I want to be." I walk towards him as Koni continues.

You ignored it because you think he's bat shit crazy. Be honest, at least.

"Have you been fucking him since you've been in charge? Or what? I know he has to know by now that you're not Koni. You two are complete opposites. If he likes Koni, you won't ever be his type," looking me head to toe as he scoffs loudly.

"What does that mean? I've spoken to him as Koni before; he could never tell the difference. We're more alike than you think, Gabe."

"So, you are fucking him? Damn. I thought you loved me, why the fuck would you take my ring if you were going to be fucking on someone else? I thought that would've stopped all that hoe shit."

He begins to pace the floor again, this time with his hand covering his face. I try to be mindful of my next words, but despite, they still slip out unfiltered.

"My hoe shit? Excuse me? I've been open and very honest with you from the very beginning. Now I'm a hoe? Why would you want to marry a hoe?" I ask, expressing every word with the movement of my hands. I rest them on my hips, awaiting his response but hear Koni's first.

Because who doesn't love a good hoe. Men are idiots.

"Man stop your bullshit. You know you like dick too much and pussy too. I love you, who you showed me before this whole situation popped off, but I could do without sharing you, even with Rocky. I hate that she's always in my face like I don't know y'all have fucked. That's a shiesty bitch for you."

See how you are shaming us by just picking any ole body to give our pussy to.

"Well, tell me how you really feel. A ring wouldn't

change me, Gabe, matter fact, wait right here." I walk away dramatically, swaying my body as I exit the room.

I go get the ring he gave me from my room. I need a break from the conversation because Koni won't shut the fuck up. It's like she becomes louder each day. She's starting to get extremely annoying. Gabe has always been very jealous, so his reaction doesn't surprise me. I don't care if he's offended or hurt at this very moment. I still feel love for him, but I've moved on from the thought of having a real-life with him. Even in the best-case scenario, he's going to prison, possibly for a long fucking time. I can't.

I lift the side of the mattress and stick my hand under to feel around for the ring. My reaches become more frantic as I come up empty-handed. It isn't here. This is where I always keep it in case Koni decides to be bold and fight her way out one day; she'll still have no sign of it. I start to search the room frantically; it should be here. I suddenly hear a lot of yelling in the living room. I can't make out the words, but it sounds like Xay. I run out to the living room to see Gabe with a gun drawn on one very pissed off looking Xay.

"And you better pull that trigger too," Xay sneers as he's walking towards Gabe. We make eye contact, as soon as he sees me, he halts in moving closer to Gabe.

Xay!! Baby, no! He's going to kill all of us. Bitch run up on him and grab it. Push him. Hell! do something! I can't help but notice how much she sounds like me right now.

"What the fuck is going on? Gabe put the gun down!" I yell, slowly moving towards him with my hands in sight.

"Bitch, you trying to set me up too? Why the fuck

would you have this motherfucker come over here when you know I'm here. I don't play this green shit Ry,' he says, waving the gun around. "It was probably you the whole time. I'm blaming Koni, but you are right, she did seem too nice to get caught up in any of this shit. But ain't shit about you sweet."

"To be clear, she didn't tell me to come over. She wasn't answering the phone, so I decided to drop in to check on her with everything being how it is, please don't hurt her." Xay pleads in a now calmer tone.

"I didn't ask you shit. I'm talking to my bitch; I'd advise you to stay out of this shit." Gabe glares at Xay.

I can't help but think how clear it is that he was never good for me. Xay has never called me out of my name, even as a term of endearment. Gabe was just the first to show me real interest; I got blinded by wanting something of my own. Koni chimes in to break my thoughts.
I don't know what you ever saw in this asshole. You chose him and somehow think you know how to make better decisions for us. Look at this shit; we're here because of you wanting freedom. This shows you never deserved it.

"Shut up! Shut up, shut up, shut up! Get out of my fucking head." I take both hands and begin to slam them against my head.

Xay begins to walk toward me, Koni still won't be quiet. *I'll never leave you alone. You will hear me until I figure out how to come back. Get used to me.*

"Do you think this is a toy?' Gabe questions as he waves the gun around in the air. 'Oh, you think I'm a joke? Take one more fucking step, and I promise it will be your last, playboy."

He lets a shot off in the ceiling, the echo from the shot scares me. I scream and drop to the floor. I look at Gabe with eyes filled with terror. He rolls his eyes, looks down at me and points the gun along with his attention back to Xay. Xay stops moving, focuses all his attention on me, but doesn't flinch.

"Baby, are you ok? What's going on?" he asks softly.

Baby? She is not your baby! It hasn't been that long for you to forget about me.

"Baby? Who the fuck are you calling baby? You really tryin' to test me. Your bitch ain't here right now, so save all that shit for if that triflin' hoe ever comes back," Gabe says with a certain blank look in his eyes.

I don't scare easily, but I know when he gets like this, consequences are no longer a thing to him. I once watched him beat a man from an inch of his life in the bar. The man had reached out and grabbed my ass as I passed. Gabe had been drinking, he approached the man, and shit went left quickly. The next day he didn't remember but also had no remorse. At the time, it turned me on thinking about how far he'd go for me. Knowing him better, I know that night was more about his ego than me.

"Gabe put the gun down, please. We can talk everything out, just please put the gun down," I plead.

"You care more about him than you do me. It was you, you lying no good bitch. What's that saying? You can't turn a hoe into a housewife! You deserve to suffer. You got rid of Koni and me just to play house with her dude. You scum bitch, now you will lose both of us." He moves the gun up towards Xay's head, with tears beginning to drop from his eyes.

Do something! Do something. We can't lose Xay. I agree. I have to do something. I begin to run towards Xay and throw my body in front of him. Except, it's not me moving.

"I do love him more. More than I will ever love you." I feel her say. I think that only I can hear this too until Gabe begins to respond.

"You bitch. I should've known a crazy bitch like you was not to be trusted. You told me you wanted to get rid of Koni and Xay, you lying ass hoe," he yells as he slightly twists his body and points the gun at me.

"I've been with Xay since college, you've only known Ryan for two years, and you put her through hell, to my understanding. If it's anyone that deserves to be exactly where they are, it's you." I feel the words again. I don't know what this is. She hasn't switched fully. How are we both here right now? How can he hear us both? I try to get rid of the feeling. I begin to concentrate on taking control.

"SHUTUP! No, Gabe. I didn't mean to say that. It wasn't me. I do love you. I really do. I'm only at this point in my life based on how much I love you. You have to know that. I just don't want anyone else to get hurt. Including you," I say, now crying, uncontrollably.

I hardly ever cry. I have no real control here. I still feel her, make it stop. Please, make it stop.

"What the fuck is going on? Am I talking to both of you? Koni? Ry? Who's in charge?" Gabe asks, lowering his gun with a look of confusion.

"Me," we say in unison.

"Let's face it, Gabe, you were just a good time. You could never compare to Xay on his worst day." Koni says in a snarky tone, almost identical to mine right now. Koni has never been the type to speak her mind. She's so passive; it's laughable. Being captive has finally taught her how to fight.

"Shut up, Koni! Gabe, don't listen to her. Please just think about this. Being charged for murder is far worse than anything you are facing right now. Please, I don't want to lose you forever. I'm sorry about all of this. Please put the gun down." I plead, going back to my attempt to calm him down. Koni is going to get us all killed.

"Fuck you and the crazy-ass other you. You need some medicine. I don't know how I ever thought this crazy shit would work," he says, his eyes glancing back and forth from me to Xay.

"Because you also need some medicine, sir. Look at how crazy you look right now. You're in here trying to shoot people over Ryan's unstable ass. You obviously don't give a fuck about anything substantial, and it shows," Koni says, sounding more and more like me with each statement.

"Shut the fuck up! How are you able to do this? Go back where you belong! You're going to get us all killed," I say, placing my hands over my ears and rocking back and forth. I have to regain control. Focus Ryan. Focus.

"You know what? You are right. None of this shit is worth it. He isn't worth the extra time they'd give me, and you aren't worth chasing. Fuck all y'all. I promise, if you did this shit to me, it will come back on you in the worse way,' he says, lowering the gun as he heads towards the door. 'Don't worry about showing up in court or anything. I don't ever want to see your crazy ass again. And wherever the ring is, you can have that petty shit," he slams the door on his way out.

Xay immediately grabs my hand and helps me up from the floor. He twists me around, squeezes me tight from behind and plants kisses on my neck. He twists me around, staring in my eyes for a full minute of silence before speaking.

"Are you ok? You two just saved my life!" he sighs as his arms tighten around my waist. I can see the gratitude in his smile.

"I– I am not ok. I could've lost you for good. I don't know what I would've done with myself." I stand on my tiptoes to kiss his lips.

"Koni?" he questions with a puzzled look on his face.

"Really? No, it's me, Ryan. I don't know what just happened there. I can't hear her anymore, either. I felt like I was going crazy. You could hear her, too, right?" I ask.

"Of course, I heard every word said. I've never seen you both in the room at the same time. But whatever happened, it saved my life and possibly yours too."

"No. You don't understand. I've been able to hear her for a few days; it didn't bother me as much before. It was like a light nagging, but I could deal with it. This shit was different Xay.", I bury my head in his chest. I feel myself on the verge of tears again. Fuck. I hate this emotional shit.

“Well, It’s over now. Things will get back on its regular track before we know it,” he says, pulling me over to the couch with him to have a seat. He begins to rub my back and shoulders and continues. ‘I could’ve taken him, you know. I was only respectful to you. If something like this happens again, I’m killing a motherfucker.” I feel his grip tighten.

“Oh yea, big talk now,’ I laugh as I side-eye him. ‘You can't fight with guns anyway. No one can."

“You can fight back if you stay prepared.’ He breaks our embrace and lifts his shirt, exposing a gun tucked in the side of his pants. The silver part is flat, wider than usual, and it has a wooden handle; I’d bet it had some power behind it. ‘You had my back, though. And so did Koni. So luckily, it didn’t get that far.”

“This is just fun for you. You get to have both. It’s cool to me, but not to Koni. She was just inciting him by being here. I could’ve done it without her.”

"How do you know she doesn't like it? Have you heard her say it? I didn't know there was a problem. She is you; y'all share the same body. I love her, and I love you too,’ he pauses and takes both of my hands in his, as to comfort me from the sting of him not being able to choose. ‘Sorry to pop in on you too. I just wanted to make sure you were good. I kept calling, and you didn't answer. I didn't mean to escalate things,” he adds as he leans in and plants a kiss in the center of my forehead.

“I’m glad you came. He was getting stupid before you got here. I had a bad feeling things were going to end ugly. I really needed you here. I'm happy it worked itself out.”

I can't hear Koni anymore. I still don't know what that whole thing was. She has gotten some emotion behind something, maybe Xay. Whatever it is, it's enough to pull her out. I need to figure this out quickly; I can't have her showing up whenever she gets too emotional. I really can't believe the audacity of Gabe. He has a right to be pissed, but that was extra. When I saw that glimpse of the old him, it was like he was beating my ass all over again. It's partially my fault; I should've known he wouldn't take any of this well before agreeing to meet him at my place. Xay did right by popping in. He was so calm the entire time. Gabe showed me he is never going to be the right one for me. Nothing longer than what we lasted. Any man in my future long term will have to love all of me; there's no compromising on that.

Like a lot of men that I've happened to un-luck upon, he only wanted me if I fit into his mold of what he thought I should be. He came after a trophy but got mad when this trophy knew her worth. He never fully accepted Koni, and although I hate her at times, she is a major part of me. I feel a sense of relief letting go of Gabe. I'll always have a love for him, but with Koni's help, I've been exposed to how truly toxic he is. I underestimated how strong she is. All those years of me protecting her, it seems like I taught her something after all. Having the constant will to fight for what she wants, knowing she can't exist under other circumstances, will give her the power to be free every-time. The battle is identical; it's up to us both to execute it.

Chapter 13

"I'm guessing Koni isn't coming back? I keep calling in hopes of speaking to her ass, but just keep ending up with you." Tia lets out a deep sigh into the phone.

"Girl, you better be glad I answer now. Keep playing, and yo' ass will be right back on my shit list,' I smack my lips for emphasis, 'You somewhere in limbo right now anyway, shit ain't sweet."

"Blah, blah. I'm shaking in my boots. You're cool too, a tad bit ghetto but still cool. I just miss Koni. You have to understand, we've been rocking since high school, I never thought I'd lose her to-' she pauses and lets out another deep sigh, "herself."

"Ghetto? Excuse me?' I pause, pull the phone away from face, roll my eyes while mumbling 'bitch' under my breath before continuing. 'Anyway, I know mostly everything about you too Tia, even with some things being a blur. I suggest that you get used to me. Koni is fighting to come back, but I am not ready to leave just yet. Either way, I'll always be around. There is no Koni without me."

"Mighty full of yourself, aren't you? Do you think you could live together? Well, you know what I mean, be together at the same time? How would it even work? Why can you turn yours on and off?"

"Years of practice and being fed up. I have always had certain triggers. Once I learned how to master that emotion that forces me out, it became easy."

"Hopefully, Koni will learn the same. If you can hear me, bitch, I'm still waiting for you to come back.", she laughs, but I know that she's serious.

"I'm about to hang up on yo' ass. What do you want?"

"Damn, I just called to talk to my stand-in best friend. I'm not going to stop calling; you should get used to me too."

"Stand in? Since when? We're cool, but Raquel would be my best friend if I just had to give the label. Understand that."

"Oh, girl shut up. I don't care who you decide to call your best friend, but it's me. I don't care what you say. How's Xay handling this change?" she asks.

"Xay is happy. Everyone is happy with me."

"Everyone was happy with Koni too," she emphasizes.

"Strike two. One more and I'm hanging up. How's Darius' fine ass?"

"Girl, I don't know if I can trust you yet, but I will cut a bitch behind fucking with mine. Do you know how long I prayed for this man? Tread lightly dear." I know she is serious.

"Girl, I don't want his ass. He's just fine as fuck. But to spare your fragile ass feelings, I won't speak on him like that moving forward."

"As long as we are clear,' she pauses, clears her throat, and continues in a much lighter tone, 'We are doing great. We've been looking for new places. That's what I was calling for actually. If you have some free time, maybe you can tag along to come view the places he'll be too busy to view with me?" she asks. I swear her mood switches as quickly as Koni and mine does.

"Really? You want me to come with you?" I ask for clarification.

"Yea, girl. You have good taste; I always loved Koni's spare bedroom. I used to joke with her all the time telling her that room was mine. It's beautiful. You're better at style than Koni, but don't tell her I said that."

"Bitch, fuck you too then.", I say, attempting to soften my tone.

"Koni?" she questions in a clear change of tone. I begin to laugh hysterically. I love fucking with her.

"Nope, yo' ass sounded scared as fuck,' I continue laughing, and Tia joins in. 'I'd love to go look at other houses with you. Wait? So y'all are looking for a house here, right?"

"Yes, most of his business operates from here, and you know it's nothing for me to catch flights for meet-ups with clients when necessary. I'm happy; I'll have my best friend close again."

"I can't tell you when Koni will be back, if ever. If I'm honest, I've been thinking about moving to a different state, sooner than later. I have a plan to get Gabriel back, and if it goes right, it'll be in our best interest to leave the state," I say, choosing to be completely transparent with her.

"I know. I meant you. You know me just as well as Koni. You know all my dirt and secrets that better go to the grave. If you think I'm going to start over with someone else, you're really crazier than I thought. And bitch, that's saying a lot. Will this plan get you hurt?" She questions in a leery tone. I know she's worried about both of us.

"No. It should only help, it's just best to move around after, just as a precaution. And yes, I do know all your dirt, but I'd never give the same advice as Koni, so just be ready."

"As long as you keep yourself safe, I'm for it. I hate that I still won't see you often, but I want you to be happy doing whatever your heart desires. I am sick of you, and this whole 'I'm not Koni' thing. You are not too much different than her. It's crazy that you've lived with her your entire life and can't see how similar you are. You're just a bit more outspoken, ghetto like I said, and obviously a damn freak. I've seen the best and worst of Koni, trust me, nothing else you do could out crazy some of the stunts that girl has pulled, and you know it too."

"Tia, a lot of her crazy is me. A lot of what you may have thought was her, has been me the entire time. You've just gotten used to both of us, without even knowing you were doing so."

"Well, good. All the more reason to stick with the same bestie. I'll text you the details of the homes I want you to look at. I have to go. Darius is on his way home, and I've been sending him nasty shit all day. Tonight is a do not disturb type of night, so I'll talk to you later. Thanks for answering."

"Uh-oh, Be nasty as I would. I'm sure I don't have to tell you that, though, that motherfucker put a ring on it for a reason. I'll see you soon."

"You better know it. Also, that ring came from several reasons. Hmmp. Put some respect on my name. I'll catch up with you soon," she laughs and hangs up the phone.

I've been talking to her daily as if she really is my best friend. Tia talks just as much shit as I do, I love it. Since Raquel made things strictly platonic, I've had time to really pay attention to her and get to know her on a level I haven't known for the last two years. She has a kid; I never even knew until this week. Her son lives with his father out of state, so she never brought him up; I also never asked. He's coming to live with her for a few months since he's getting older. It's crazy how much sex has clouded my vision when it comes to her. How could I not know the only female I considered a friend until recently, has a whole kid? She'd do anything for me; I never realized just how great of a friend she's always been to me. I don't deserve her.

It's been about a week since the incident with Gabe. I haven't spoken to him since. I'm supposed to meet with Gabriel later today to go ahead and switch all his businesses in my name, but I have a surprise for him. I know he trusts me, that's his biggest mistake yet. He should know better than to trust anyone. I've had a few visits with Dr. Rainey, and I'm feeling that I'm starting to grasp the concept that we are truly the same person. I'm finally coming to terms with it all. I begin to test the camera in my office to make sure it's still working. It is. Koni having this camera installed, came in handy after all. I don't think she has checked them once since she had them installed. She hardly follows through with anything. As I'm playing around with the camera software on my laptop, Shelly buzzes over the intercom.

"Koni, my man is here to see you,' she giggles, 'Girl, it feels so good to say that. He's a little early, are you ready for him?"

"I'm glad you can say it. Go ahead, send your man back," I say. Who am I to take her small thrill away. She giggles again and goes silent as I hear a knock on my door. Gabriel opens it and walks in without me having to invite him back.

"Koni, so good to see you as always," he says as he pushes the door back closed.

"The pleasure is all mine today. Please, come in." He walks into my office; I close the door behind him. I can't help but still admire his style. He has his dreads down today which helps set off his look. The deep red and orange tones in his silk, long sleeve, button-down top draws me in immediately. He's wearing it with the top three buttons undone, exposing his salt and pepper curly chest hair. He has it paired it with tan slacks and a nice pair of brownish-orange Cole Hans. I take it all in; sometimes it's hard to remember how triflin' his fine ass is. I'm glad I never met him as Gabe's father early on, I definitely would've fucked him and had no regret about it. I regret not getting the opportunity before this. If this doesn't go as planned, I can't say I'd fully regret meeting him. He sits in the empty seat in front of my desk. I watch as he shuffles through his briefcase until he pulls out a black and gold folder.

"Here is a list of every owner's name, length of business, and how much they are paying to get covered per month. I also included my price list for hiding anything other than the amounts originally agreed on. Everything you need to know is here. It's a cheat book; make it easy for you. I'd suggest you follow it because the risks get higher the more money they need you to handle," he says as he nods his head and waves his hand over the folder, urging me to have a look.

"Ok, I really appreciate you putting all of this together. Before we make things official, mind if I pick your brain a bit?" I ask, ignoring his silent request. It's enough of a task trying not to tell him what I think about him right now.

"Go ahead; you're doing me a solid. I'll answer whatever you need." He throws a cocky smile my way, eager to give me the game.

"How long have you been with your clients? I'm surprised they all agreed since they built their trust with you. I'm scared of how they'll interact with me. I need your best tips to thrive in this."

"Baby girl, you are going to do fine. The first person I started doing it for was Rico. He's the first person on the list if you look in your folder. I have every year on paper, just for security purposes. Rico was one of my corner boys for a long time," he pauses and uncomfortably clears his throat, "well, that is when I was into that shit. When I went to jail, he held shit down. When I got out, I told him I wanted to be legit. Once my attempt at that failed, I went back, asking what other options he had for me that aren't on the street.

"He knew I was good with money and hiding shit, so he came to me about having extra funds that need to look like they are legit, and thus, my business was born. That was seven years ago. Now, I have more money than I need, and I can afford to be fully on the up and up for the rest of my life. Don't worry too much; they won't have any problem listening to or working with a woman as beautiful as yourself. Don't get anyone involved in your business or their business and trust me; they'll love you," He says, his dreads cascading down his shoulders as he tilts his head to the side and smiles to offer reassurance.

"I'm just a little scared. You've been doing this for that long and managed to come out clean. Even with the whole Gabe thing, that was genius. I don't know if I have someone who can take the fall for me if shit goes crazy."

"Gabe knew what he was getting into by dealing with any of it. It's just his time to sit. I hated for it to all fall on him, but better him than me. Thanks again for helping with that lil situation. You're smart; you helped me out of mine, so I know you'll figure it out if things ever get to that point with your own."

"I never plan for them to. What happens when I want to stop? I only want to do this for two years, tops," I say, holding up my index and middle finger to stress not having any interest in making this a long-term career or hustle.

"I know you'll be able to find someone in your circle that wants to be on the money team or needs the money. Once you build that trust with my clients, they'll understand when it's time to leave the game, even if it's only two years."

"You said you didn't know if they'd understand when you did it, and you've known them for way longer."

"Exactly. They were mostly on the fence with me because I have so much dirt on them that it was best to keep me in the pocket. But since I'm getting out of this altogether, all of their dirt will die with me. You will only know them in a business sense; your financial background also looks good on paper; they will give you more trust than they ever gave me."

I can tell he's trying to ensure that I keep up my end of our deal. I reach over to the desk, pick up the folder and start to thumb through it. It's surprisingly well organized; it lists how much he's charged for each client since they began to use his services; making a note of personality traits, listing past problems they've had as well as going out of the way to include a brief profile of each client. As I flip a little more, I also come across a mega list of every other business client they have, even the ones he doesn't manage. This folder is gold and just what I needed.

"I still feel bad about Gabe. I don't know if I'm over him yet," I lower my eyes, drop my head and begin to wipe away at phantom tears.

"Koni, no offense, but you gone have to get that bitch shit out of your system in this game. You have to do whatever to protect you, fuck everyone else, and I do mean everyone." He looks down and checks his watch, straightens his cufflinks, looks back up at me and smiles as if he's waiting for a response.

"Fuck everyone else, huh?" I question, putting the folder in a file cabinet behind my desk and turning back to look at him, 'Well, that's my plan exactly. Starting with you."

"Starting with me? What does that mean?" His brows wrinkle.

"It means you are one dirty motherfucker, and I can be just as dirty. That shit with Gabe was whack. You should've gotten all your facts straight before making a deal with me."

"Facts? Bitch stop playing with me. You sound mighty different today. Don't start no bullshit; this is a good deal. You need to just take it."

It shocked me a little to hear him call me out of my name. Even with Gabe telling me all the trifling shit over time, he's been nothing but respectful since Koni or I have encountered him. I sit down in my chair and smirk as I look over at him.

"Yes, your motherfucking facts. I'm not Koni; I'm Ryan. Ryan, who was engaged to your son. Ryan, who never would've done that shit to him. Your deal was with Koni, not me."

"What the fuck are you talking about? You have a fucking identical twin? Where is Koni?" he raises his voice, his expressions showing me his confusion is now being replaced by anger. I tilt my head back and begin to laugh as I pick up my phone and begin to play back our conversation. He gets up, leans over my desk and reaches for the phone.

"Not so fast, this isn't the only thing recording. Look up.' I point to the camera I set up in the office. 'Take one more step, and I won't tell you your only option to get out of this." He stops and balls his fists as he lowers his hands to his sides.

"What the fuck do you want? Whatever you and your sister got going, ain't my beef. I didn't know; I thought he was thinking about asking you. I didn't know shit about you even having a twin."

"I don't have a fucking twin,' I roll my eyes, annoyed with his cluelessness. 'I want money, or you will serve your own time. It's enough here to even get Gabe off completely," I taunt, still smirking.

"Money?! I should've known not to trust a bitch. You're just a gold-digging hoe, just like these regular hood hoes,' He yells. He slowly rubs his hands together as he sits back down. "Everything has its price, though. I can't be mad at how you pimped this. How much?" he asks calmly.

"I won't even be greedy. I want 500,000. That's nothing to you. Remember, Koni handled your finances, so I've been over every inch." I smile and rub my hands together to mock him.

"That is cheap compared to what you have on the table. Maybe that shit wasn't for you anyway," he shakes his head, seeming disappointed.

"750,000, since you're so fucking cocky. And it's non-negotiable."

"How do I know that you won't just turn me in anyway. Or that your sister won't? What do I get as security?"

"Koni looks like me because she is me. To be clear, we share the same body. Stop fucking calling her my sister. In good sportsmanship, I'll delete the recording, and the tape is video only, no audio. Other than that, all you'll have is my word. Take it or leave it," I lean forward and rest both elbows on the desk.

"Crazy bitch. I should've never listened to the shit, Gabe suggested. That boy is always fucking up. Looks like I don't really have a choice. But I swear to God if you fuck me over, I'll be the last one you ever fuck over." He lifts his hand, shapes his fingers like a gun and does a shooting motion.

"Save your tough guy shit. I don't give a fuck. I need it in an hour. You can bring it back; if not, I'll turn all of this over to the detectives. You have a weak spot; you exposed it by turning on your own son. You'll decide what you want when you leave here, but I don't think you will prove me any wrong." I stand up and begin walking towards the door.

"I hope you plan on leaving town with that money because you chose the wrong bridge to burn," he says, standing from the chair.

"Your bridge was bound to ignite naturally, anyway. You have an hour starting now,' I say, moving my hand in a sweeping motion toward the door. 'I hope to see you soon, Mr. Grove."

He walks over, opens the door and makes sure to stop to stare at me. I turn to point at the camera, while simultaneously waving my phone in the air. He slams the door on the way out. I should still make him pay for his lack of morals, but money needs to be in hand first.

I can understand a lot of grimy things but fucking over family isn't one. I do want his money. If I turn him in, Gabe will be free, but I want Xay. I've never had anyone so interested in who I really am. Gabe doesn't really have shit going for himself besides what his father has given him. He doesn't know how to talk to me unless he knows he's about to fuck. Koni is right; it's my fault for ever choosing him. Shelly barges into the office, opening the door so hard it bounced back off the wall.

"Excuse me? Was that necessary?"

"Yes, it was. What the fuck is Gabriel talking about? You're blackmailing him? Then he said something about you having multiple personalities, did I hear him right?"

"Shelly, this is a private matter and none of your concern. He owes me money. It's nothing more and nothing less."

"Owes you money for what? He always pays you on time! He even told me he gave you ten thousand dollars the first time he met you. I told him that was the problem. He showed your greedy ass too quickly what you could get out of him." She moves in closer to my desk.

"You mean the same reason you're fucking him. Shelly, this isn't your business; watch yourself. He's a big boy; I think he can handle this fine," I wave my hands in a shooing motion.

"Koni, or whoever the fuck you are, I won't let anyone fuck him over. You need to leave him out of whatever beef. You already knew what he did when you took him on as a client. But to try to blackmail him? This ain't right," she crosses her arms and tucks them in front of her.

"Shelly, shut the fuck up. You don't know the background, so you really shouldn't be speaking on this. I've always liked you, just stay out of this shit and keep getting your paycheck."

"What is that supposed to mean? Is that a threat? I don't need this job anymore. Gabriel spoils me more than Xay could ever do with you," pursing her lips as she rolls her eyes.

"Damn, do you have a ring? The way you riding for this man that you've only been fucking for what? Three weeks now? Please have several seats," I stand from my desk and walk towards her.

"Koni, I'm leaving when Gabriel comes back. I can no longer work for you," she begins to back away towards the door. I stop, as not to cause fear.

"You're going to sacrifice your money over the hopes of the next motherfucker footing your bills? I thought you had more sense than that. I'd suggest you wait this out. Once Gabe comes back, I won't be with this company much longer anyway. Black woman to black woman, I know other assistant jobs don't pay this well, and it's hard to get on with no degree in this field. Stay. I will be out of your life sooner than you think."

"Black woman to black woman? You are not my sis, so stop acting like you give a damn about me. I thought I liked the recent change in you, but now? I want the old Koni back; she'd never do anything this grimy."

"You talk too damn much and don't listen enough. Do what you want girl; it's no longer my concern. Now, please close my door. You're free to leave." She opens her mouth as if she is about to say something else but stops, turns around and slams the door on her way out.

Gabriel deserves everything coming his way. If Shelly wants to go down with him, she can be my guest. I pick up the phone to call Xay.

"Hey, Ry, what's up? You never call me through the day. Are you ok?"

"I am more than ok. I just wanted to run something by you to see how you'd feel."

"Ok, what is it?"

"How would you feel about moving away with me?"

"Moving away? Away to where baby?"

"It honestly doesn't matter, somewhere beautiful. I'm open to suggestions; I just want to be gone by the end of the month."

"The end of the month? That's less than two weeks, Ry? What are we going to do for money? You don't even have a place in mind? What's all of this about?"

"So, you're not down with it? I have the money covered. I'll have enough for us to live comfortably, and even enough to start our own businesses. I just need to leave."

"How'd you get that much money? Why are you just now talking to me about it if it's something that's been on your mind? Are you sure you're ok? This sounds far from it," his voice lowers. I know he's at work and doesn't want others in our business.

"Yes, Xay, I'm fine. You're asking so many questions, just forget that I asked. Shit," I sigh deeply into the phone.

"Don't be like that. I will follow you anywhere; I'm just trying to figure it all out. Now isn't the best time to really talk about it."

"We'll talk more in detail when I get off. I just need to know if you're down or not?"

"I can't see my life without you. You know I've wanted to be completely self-sufficient for a while now. This sounds like the move we've both been waiting for. I'm always down with you baby, we'll discuss the details later like you said, but I'm with you every step of the way."

"Xay, I love you."

"I love you too, Ryan. This shit is forever, no matter what."

"No matter what," I repeat and hang up the phone.

I can hear a lot of movement outside of my door. I don't care to inquire about what Shelly has going. I get up, remove the folder from my file cabinet and make copies of each page before putting the copies back in the cabinet and laying the folder on my desk. I compose an email and letter to be sent out to all my clients. In the letter, I thank them for their continued support and for choosing me. I go on to tell them this will be my last month handling the accounts. I will be passing them all over to Nicole; even with her hating on me, I still would rather give them over to her. The clients likely want to continue to work with a woman with a good head on her shoulder. Nicole still fits that description.

I feel the sadness creeping upon me; I really do love Koni's clients. They have been so good to us over the years and getting to handle them myself has really impacted my business skills. I never had practice working anywhere, I always let Koni do that for us. If no one else understands, they'll understand taking an opportunity when it knocks at the door. I also write out my resignation letter. After I complete all of the emails and put each letter in envelopes, I pack up things on my desk. Once he brings this money back, I have no plans on returning to this office. I hear a knock on my door and pause my packing to get it. I walk over and pull the door open.

"I see you decided it was in your best interest to come back after all," I smile.

Gabriel stares at me with a smug look on his face. If looks could kill, I'd be one dead bitch. He pulls a thick envelope out of his pocket. It's black with a gold sticker, just like the one I saw in Koni's room several months back. He hands it over. I take the envelope from him, open it and begin to flip through the stacks of money.

"No need to count it; it's all there," he pushes his way past me and walks into the office.

"Does that work when people tell you that about your money?' I ask, raising one eyebrow as I turn to look at him while simultaneously kicking the door shut with my foot. He just stares and doesn't say a word. 'That's what I thought. But no worries, it won't take too long. I walk over to the shelf and begin to unwrap each 100k and place it in my money counter. Each one is accurate; seven hundred and fifty thousand dollars in hand. I could've gotten him for much more, but I only requested what it would take to start over somewhere new. I've never touched this much money at one time. I turn back to Gabriel and smile.

"It pays to be in position. I was going to let this all go and just tell you that I was no longer interested in taking over your business because I have too much to lose, but this plan seemed more appropriate after Gabe paid a visit to my home based on the information you told him. You'll truly do anything to stay out of the heat. You should've never told Gabe it was me especially since it was all your fucking idea, I'm sure. Koni didn't come up with this shit on her own."

"I'm not saying shit else to you. Can I have the recording? And I need to watch you delete the audio now," He says, sounding annoyed.

I walk over to my desk, pull an SD card out of the camera and hand it over to him. He watches as I pick up my phone, play the recording back and delete it from my files. I hand over my phone so that he can verify that it's gone. He looks through it, clicking into other recordings just to be sure.

"You will get what's coming to you. No one plays me and gets away with it. I'll just leave it at that," he tosses my phone back on the desk.

"Maybe I'm your karma finally catching up to you. Did you ever think of it like that? Do what you must, Gabriel. I'm not scared of you. Your clients won't be too happy that you shared all of their information with me or if I tell them you keep this detailed folder of everything they've ever hidden with you. Seems pretty Narc like if you ask me."

"You win, are you happy now? I need the folder back too since you won't be using it. This is the last time I'll ever try to look out for a bitch again. Just stay the fuck out of my life, and I'll do the same," he picks the folder up off my desk.

"Deal Mr. Grove. It was a pleasure meeting and doing business with you," I smile and extend my hand for a shake. He looks at me and begins to shake his head in disgust.

"Go fuck yourself," he walks out the door, and I hear him yell at Shelly to come on.

I walk out and see that they're both gone. Good riddance. I finish packing up the office. I'm going to miss this place, just a little. I'm sure Koni will miss it a little too. She always seemed to hate having to work; it doesn't reflect in the amount of shit she has in this office. It almost looks like an extension to her bedroom. I can tell she hand-picked all the decorations; the next associate who gets this office will be grateful. I leave the letter of resignation on the desk along with the office keys and badge. I walk out with the basic essentials packed in a box, not so much as glancing back once on my way out.

Chapter 14

I place my hand under the messy cream satin sheets of his California King bed to feel around for my bra while still trying to catch my breath. I feel a row of clasps hit my fingertips, I grab the bra and begin to slide it up my arms. I feel his hand reach over to clasps the back for me.

"What happened today to make you want to leave so last minute? Talk to me." Xay asks as he finishes with the last hook. I turn around to look for my thong and get lost in admiring him. His chocolate skin is glistening from the work he just put in.

"Xay, nothing happened. One of Koni's clients gave me a large bonus. That combined with my savings, we'll be set for a while. We're both tired of working in our career fields already. We're still young, why not take this opportunity. I believe in us; nothing changed today except for finally having the money." I look directly in his eyes and lick my lips as I begin to stroke his goatee.

He leans in and kisses my neck before getting up and starting to get dressed. I don't want him to feel any way about me helping Gabe out, so I just omit it. He shouldn't have to think about if I still have feelings for Gabe. I do. I will deeply miss him always.

"I have decent savings myself. The burden doesn't have to fall fully on you. Koni mentioned wanting to move a while back. We just never acted on it. Where do you want to go?"

"I thought maybe Arkansas originally, it has such beautiful scenery. But I don't think I'm ready to settle there just yet. What do you think about Colorado? Or I'm open to places you'd think we could thrive. Preferably, low key."

"Since when are you low key? Maybe Koni, but you?" He lifts his brow, gives a judgment heavy stare and begins to laugh.

"Oh, so what am I? Maybe she's wearing off on me. I understand her more than I ever have. I'm ready for a nice restart."

"Well, I don't know if I'm sold on Colorado. Maybe move to the far east side of the map. Something like Maine? I'm down either way. We'll compare ideas and decide tomorrow. And it sounds like a good thing, being in tune with her. I like the 'low-key' Ry, too. I'm with you through whatever if you haven't figured that out yet." I watch as he moves around his bedroom, looking for his keys. He always misplaces them.

"I'll be visiting Dr. Rainey in the morning. One last visit before we go. I also hired a moving company earlier for both of our spaces. We need to decide tonight; they'll be coming to pack both places for the next two days. I know this is sudden but after that Gabe incident, I've been shook and ready to go."

"Ok, we'll figure it out tonight, after dinner,' he stops and puts his hands on his head, 'That is if I ever get to it." He sighs loudly from frustration.

"I keep trying to figure out how I got so lucky,' I pause and begin to giggle, 'They're on your top shelf in your closet. I can see them from here."

I point my finger towards his keys. He begins to shake his head as he walks over and picks them up and walks back toward me. He leans down and kisses my forehead.

"I'll be right back; do you want any extra sauce? Or anything else while I'm out?"

"Maybe a bottle of wine for Round Two later?" I tease.

I tug on his pants and lick my tongue out. He laughs, nods his head and walks out the door. Xay is so perfect, attentive, easy to talk to, loving yet aggressive. He has dealt with both of us with nothing but love. He accepts us for who we are, individually and together. He's making me soft. I trust him. I've never trusted anyone, not even myself. I'm honored he chose us– happy that Koni allowed him to choose us. I would have never forgiven myself if I fucked this up with my delusions about Gabe. He gives us peace; that's what we've always needed.

"You're moving? But we've been doing so good, Ryan. I've enjoyed getting to know you on your own," Dr. Rainey says.

"I've enjoyed this process more than I thought, but I

have to leave. I can't take the risk of Gabriel or Gabe sending someone. They know where I live and work. Well, worked," I say, my eyes locked on her hair. I haven't been able to take my eyes off her beautifully curled ginger fro. I'm going to miss getting to work with her.

"Are you scared that he's going to try to retaliate? What's the rush?" she frowns and peers over the edge of her notebook.

"Yes, I am scared that he will try to ruin me. Either by killing me, someone I love or at the very least, my reputation. I think it'd be better to start somewhere new." I shuffle uneasily on her couch.

"Why don't you just call the police? I think it'd be best for your safety."

"I can't. I mayor may not have gotten a lot of money from him in exchange for secrecy.', I pause, avoiding eye contact with her. 'I have something in mind to get Gabriel, though. I'm not going to the Police. I'm not a police ass bitch. I'm focused on this move right now; I can't be caught up in any of that. Once I'm gone, I'm out for a long while." I tilt my head back and close my eyes.

"I understand. Going back to what you said before; Why does he, attempting to ruin your reputation bother you? How would he be able to ruin it? By speaking on Koni?" she asks as she begins scribbling in her notebook. I wish she would just get rid of the damn thing all together.

"No. By speaking on Koni incorrectly. I don't want him to make us come off as crazy." I correct her.

"What do you want to come off as?"

"Not crazy."
We're not crazy! Fuck. Here she comes.

"I understand that. I don't think you're crazy. I think you're highly intelligent. I'm curious as to what you'd like the world to understand. You mentioned him speaking incorrectly on Koni? What is the correct way?"

"I don't want them to see us as crazy. We're strong when we're under control. Really, I'm modest; we're brilliant. I feel we're in a good place to learn how. I understand more than I ever have, and I believe so does Koni. I've begun to feel her. I know her thoughts; I can even tell when we're about to switch. Sometimes I still have small gaps of time I don't remember, but I can prevent it most times."

You only think that because I let you. I hear her taunt me.

"Shh." I accidentally utter out-loud. Dr. Rainey begins to stare at me with a puzzled look on her face.

"Was that for Koni? What is she saying?", she begins scribbling on her pad again, her hand moving so fast it looks robotic. I sigh and roll my eyes. She repeats her question.

"She thinks she's in control still. She's not strong enough to come and go when she wants but she won't shut up about it." I roll my eyes again.

"You said she has been back a few times since our last visit, right? Sounds like she's getting stronger." She puts her notebook down, walks toward her desk and begins to fondle through her file cabinet.

"Maybe, but not enough. With her, it's still all emotion–" I get quiet. I can feel it.

"Ryan? Are you ok?" Dr. Rainey stops shuffling through papers and snaps her fingers together repeatedly.

"I'm scared. I'm so tired of them fighting.", I hear an unrecognizable child-like voice echo. I'm not sure what it is.

"Hello?" Dr. Rainey looks stunned. She walks over and begins to hover over me. "Tired of who fighting?" Before I can respond, I hear the child again.

"They never get along. It's too noisy in there," tears begin to roll down my face. I involuntarily place my thumb in my mouth. I feel the room closing in. I want to tune out but I can't for some reason. I try to practice breathing techniques like Koni does when she usually starts feeling like this. I can't control the breaths.

"I don't like noisy places, either. What's your name, sweetheart?" Dr, Rainey ask as she looks over at me, squints her eyes, tilts her head and reaches for her notebook and pen.

I don't know why she's looking at me. I feel the tears increase. My heart feels like it's going to explode. I hear silence and finally feel myself being able to control my breaths. That didn't feel like Koni. I get the feeling as if we are about to switch again. What the fuck?

"Are you still with me?" Dr. Rainey reaches down and touches my shoulder.

"I'm ok. I don't know why she tests me like this." I hear

the proper voice echo. Now, this feels like Koni. I'm so exhausted. I don't try to fight her anymore. I go inward and tune out.

"Who tests you? Ryan and Koni?" she asks, going back through her notebook to read something she's written.

"And? What are you talking about? It's been cool getting to sit back in these sessions while you get Ryan in her feelings. I've learned so much. It has also helped me realize a major part of my issue. I never could control my emotions. I allowed them to rule me, and I suffered greatly because of it."

"Koni? You've been gone for quite some time, as far as I know. My last few sessions have been with Ryan. However, I thought I was just speaking to someone else? You mentioned being tired of hearing them fight? Is everything ok?"

"Tired of who fighting? You must've misheard me. I can feel Ryan when I'm inside too now. I have studied myself in a way I didn't think I could, thanks to you. I finally understand what you were telling me from the beginning. I'll always lose fighting against myself."

"Yes, exactly. Embracing who you are, even if it changes frequently, is the most important task of getting through this in a healthy manner.", she pauses and gives a questioning look. "This may seem random to you, but do you suck your thumb?"

"What? Why ask me that? When have you ever seen me suck my thumb? I haven't done that since I was nine.' I cut my eyes over to her and continue, 'And you're right. I've been so at ease. I've been interacting and learning that I could speak from anger. That's the only time I really know she can hear me. But I was so caught up on sulking; I wasn't thinking and feeling logical. Now I have it down."

"How does it feel when you switch? You can hear what's she's saying? Can you see everything? Like watching television?"

"Sort of. It feels like I'm watching a really great show staring me, but I don't have control of the script, so although it looks just like me, it's nothing like me. I can hear when I tune in, but it's fuzzy. Like if I went to recall the conversations had while Ryan, it's unclear and garbled. The memory will seem distant because it's not my own." I try to sum it up as best as I can.

"If you can switch when you want, why are you allowing her to be Ryan?"

"At first, I wasn't allowing anything. I had lost control. Now, I've learned to manage my feelings, and use the negative feelings to remind me of freedom and how to fight when I want it. Right now, she needs to be free, and I need her to be as well. Problems come from trying to shut her out."

"How does it make you feel that she's taken over as you? Picked up with Xay and Tia. She told me about the engagement; you even let her have that."

"I came out for Tia that night. I let her get to know her because she needs to. It's clear she's not going anywhere the same with Xay. She needed to be herself with him; he needed to test if he could handle the reality of all of this. Being completely transparent, I get jealous if I tune in while she's screwing Xay. It's hard to know it's not me. To the world, she is me; we all have to get used to her."

"One more question,' she pauses and reaches over to her tape recorder, making sure it was still on. "Have you ever heard more than just Ryan in there?" she points to my head.

"Never. It's just us. I think I'd know if it were more. One is already hard to deal with. Please don't wish more on me."

"I'm sorry. It's just a clarification question; I didn't mean to offend. This sounds like what we've been working toward. I'm happy that you changed your outlook on this. You seem to be doing well," she reaches back over and stops the recorder.

"I am. I'm glad I started seeing you again. This has been one long ride, and I can't thank you enough. Is it ok if I call you when I leave until I'm able to find a new therapist?" I ask, nervously fondling with the pillows sitting on her couch.

"Of course. Please do! Depending on what area you're moving to, I may be able to recommend someone for you." she gets up and walks back towards her desk.

"We decided on Colorado for our business purposes. We found a nice Airbnb to get us started. We've hired movers, and we'll be there by the end of the week. It's going to take some getting used to, but I'm ready for this new adventure together."

"So, Colorado, as your new forever home or are you going to try a few different places?" she asks as she tears a page out of her notebook and scribbles down a few names and numbers.

"Colorado, until we get tired of it. I won't say forever. We have plans to buy land in Arkansas too, somewhere to settle down when we get bored and decide to create and focus on family. I hope that's possible."

"Well, I know a few therapists located in both, so please be in touch. Thank you for allowing me the pleasure to work with you. I wish you nothing but the best. Be safe. All of you.", she hands over the list of therapists.

"Thank you again.' I walk over to her and hug her. 'For everything."

I usually only shake her hand or wave, but a hug feels more appropriate for a goodbye. I walk out of her office and head home to supervise the movers. On my way home, I stop by the bar; it's finally back open. I walk in happy to see Rocky behind the bar. It's empty besides one other person. I walk over to the bar and have a seat. Rocky begins to walk towards me.

"Hey, Ry! What brings you in here?" she smiles.

"It's Koni. I'm happy I found you here."

"You're back? I've been back every day since the reopen. Even you should know that I'm gone get this money. You can never have too much," she says, less excited that it's me. Her smile drops into a straight face.

"For a little while, yes. I just have to do this before I go. We're moving out of state. I'm sure Ryan will want to keep your friendship and will reach out when she decides; I wouldn't mind keeping in touch either. But today, I'm here for business."

"Business? What business do we have?" she scoffs as she pouts her lips and gives me a side-eye.

"We don't. I need you to do me a favor. But you can't speak on it once it's done. I need you to get a package to Gabe's lawyer in two days. I can't say too much, but it will help him. Please, I need this to be quick and discreet," I say, lowering my voice as a precaution. I pull the black and gold envelope from Gabriel out, what a perfect way to get reuse from it.

"What? What is it? Something to help get him off? Why would you help him? I thought you were trying to get rid of him? He thinks you're the one that set him up, remember?" she questions and rolls her eyes.

"Change of heart. I'm better than who I let myself be for a moment. I need to make it right. I'm going to leave this with you. Please, get it to him. Don't mention it to anyone, especially Gabriel." I pass the envelope to her. She just stares for a minute, then takes it and slips it in her bag under the bar.

"I'll drop it off. But only for Gabe. Gabriel doesn't deserve him as a son. I hope this really does help and not hurt him more."

"If he has a half-decent lawyer, it will. If he doesn't, I'll get him one if he just says the word. Please let him know if he doesn't already have it situated. Thank you for everything." I reach my hand out to shake hers. She leaves my hand hanging there and begins to walk from behind the bar.

"If Ry doesn't keep in touch, you better make sure you do. Bye Koni.", she gets to my chair and reaches out for a hug. I lean in, hug her and watch her smile as she walks towards the only other person here. I leave and head home.

I pull into my driveway and see a large moving van parked on the lawn of all places. The nerve of them! I get out of my car and walk inside. I see one mover playing with Alexa with his feet kicked up on my suede couch, another in my refrigerator and the last one was taking a shower.

A fucking shower? Oh, hell no.

She's pissed. I can feel that she's on her way. My anxiety would never allow me to say the things she says to people, even at this point. I finally understand, we both have our place. She's important, but so am I. She saves me from my anxiety. She fights my depression; She stands up for me. I held us together for a long time, I've finally come around to the idea of sharing; releasing my need to control everything. I believe Ryan has too. She's not too bad at keeping everything running smoothly. She's able to pretend so well, everything seems as if it was before I was ever interrupted, finally, back in perfect harmony.

Appearing Act

Sometimes, I wish you'd disappear. Or at least give me notice when you're on your way. I'm still not sure of what to even call you. It's nothing like the movies portray.

We don't have different names or accents. Only different feelings and different memories. I could never tell your story, even though you are a part of me. So much so, they keep telling me that you...are me.

The first time I remember you, was 6th grade. I got into a fight and couldn't remember a thing. I just know they said it was me. But I... only remember the anger building. I swear it wasn't really me.

Since then, you pop in and out whenever I need protection. More recently you showed your face again, in a way that I couldn't ignore.

Again, I swore it wasn't me.
And I believed it whole-heartedly.

Sitting there writing my statement, I drew a blank. I had a gap of time that I couldn't remember, but I filled it in anyway.

It wasn't until they let me go, that I was able to see. It had to be you because it sure wasn't me. I mean, I'd never stab someone repeatedly.

I went to seek help, and that's when I knew. I replayed my entire life and am still in denial about what's true. All I can focus on now is if it's more than just you.

Epilogue

"What do you think about this one?" he says, holding out a red heart-shaped mouth gag.

"We already have a few gags we haven't used yet. How about this?" I hold out a cutely packaged app-controlled cock ring as a counteroffer.

He takes it from my hands and begins reading.

"That doesn't sound like a bad time. We could use it with the app-controlled vibrator next time we have a date night. I can watch your expressions from across the table. My dick is getting hard thinking about it, "he says, reaching down to adjust his pants. I look down and see that his pants are beginning to rise in that area. I run my hand over his pants in a circular motion, outlining the tip. He pushes my hands away.

"I'd love that; you know I'd give you a good show too. Let's get this one. I can't believe it's been five years since we've been in a relationship."

"I can. Think about all the unused toys we still have from each month. I love that we started this tradition. We'll have more toys than we know what to do, within a few years."

"I'm sure you and Ryan will have gone through them all before that point. Besides, who says you're going to be around that long?" I lift my eyebrow and give him a side-eye. He begins to side-eye me back. I tilt my head back and laugh obnoxiously.

"Honestly, I've wanted to talk to you about something important. I'm ready, and I need to know if we're on the same page. All of us."

"Talk about what?" I feel my nerves begin to creep up on me. That statement always makes me uneasy.

"Marriage. I can't imagine living without you or Ryan. I love you. Both of you. I need to figure out where we all stand."

We stare at each other for a few moments in silence. He picked a weird place to bring this up. Although, we are the only two in the entire store, aside from the cashier. This is basically a proposal in a damn sex shop.

"Xay, you know I've wanted this since we reunited after college. I knew then you'd be my husband. And I think I've gotten in a comfortable enough space to know that Ryan wants the same. We both love you and have fun with you. You accept us for who we are at all times. You never neglected us or skipped a beat when all the crazy shit hit the fan. If you aren't my husband, we'll never marry," I reassure.

"Oh, really? Well, I know I was talking to Ryan one day, and she was so anti wedding I just assumed she never wanted to get married, so I've been sitting on it. I want it to be right for all of us," he begins to fidget with the packaging of the toy nervously.

"I'm pretty anti wedding myself. I feel it's a waste of time and money. The whole ordeals are pretty stressful. I thought I wanted one for so long—honestly, all the way up until we moved here. We don't have that many people to invite, and I feel it should be a private celebration. I'd even consider eloping, like Tia and Darius did."

"I thought you were upset that she eloped? I heard your mouth for two weeks straight after she told you," he chuckles.

"I wasn't upset with the idea of eloping. I was only upset that she had me flying back and forth to plan it, only for our hard work to go to waste. It would've been beautiful."

"So, let's do it then. Let's elope," he says, smiling and holding his arms out.

"Xay, are you serious?"

"Let's go to the courthouse today. I have a ring for you that I picked out before I met Ryan. I think you'll love it, but we can always exchange it if you both don't agree on it. I want to still give you a wedding one day soon, but the sooner you're my wife, the better.

"You got me a ring? Why'd you wait? She accepted a proposal without me; I would've said yes a long time ago." I smile, reach out and hug him tight.

"I thought it was best to let you sort everything out. Especially finding out about Gabe. I didn't know what you wanted, and I wanted to allow time for you to choose."

"I've always wanted you. I'm so happy! Let's go now." I put the toy down and begin to walk towards the door of the adult novelty store. He pulls my arm back toward him.

"No need to break tradition. Let's still buy our toy. We did make it another month. We'll swing by the house to get the ring and head to the courthouse after this."

"You're right. After today, we'll be celebrating months of marriage instead. We're can use them tonight."

"Tonight, you'll be my wife. We're going to go all out."

"I know a better idea, let's use it during the ceremony. I don't care what the ring looks like, to be honest; I just want the moment to be memorable."

"That's not a bad idea Ry, I'd love to hear you moan I do instead.", he leans in and squeezes my butt and holds his tongue out. I meet him with my tongue; we kiss deeply, yet nasty. I feel myself get a little wet between my thighs.

"You know I'm not Ryan. Stop playing. But, of course, you would, that better double for me. I'm the last freak you'll ever get to be with," I say, walking towards the front of the store, dragging his hand behind me.

"Trust me; you two are all the freak I need. I doubt I ever get bored with you all."

"We love you too, Xay. Let's pay for this and get to changing my last name already. Come on."

I drag him towards the check-out where the cashier is. We check out quickly and make our way back to our home. Xay gets out of the car and runs in while I sit and admire our new home from the carport. It is beautiful. It's a three-story A-frame home. Half of which is furnished to my liking in dark neutral tones, the other is to Ryan's, in gold and white. We have a pool, a garden, a tennis court, and most importantly, our nearest neighbor lives ten miles away. The lawn is so green it looks fake. We have a beautiful tree in front of the home that gets cut into the shape of three inter-twined hearts every two weeks, which is the perfect symbol for us. He comes back out, gets in and begins to drive to the courthouse.

"Let me see it. Come on, I want to see it now." I whine and start patting towards his pockets. He 'shoos' me away with one hand.

"Baby, I'll show you when we get there. I know you'll love it. I don't know about Ryan, though."

"She doesn't have to love it. She'll be ok. Our tastes aren't the same anyway. You chose it for me; I want it." I lean back over to my seat, "but I will wait until we get there. I can't believe we're really doing it."

"I can." Xay takes his eyes off the road, glances over at me and smiles before turning back to the road. I reach over and grab his hand, cherishing this last ride as boyfriend and girlfriend. I look out the window and feel a sense of calm-ness take over my body. I'm thankful for being at this point after everything that has happened. I begin to reflect on how crazy the last few months have been.

It's almost been a year since that night at the bar. Although I was upset about how things were going then, I couldn't have wished for a different outcome in my wildest dreams. Once Gabe was released from prison after the discovery of the videotaped conversation in my old office, his lawyer got him off. He called to thank me and to apologize for that whole incident with him and Xay. Gabriel went on the run and into hiding as soon as he got word there was a warrant out for his arrest. I read in the news that most of his clients were arrested and charged with several crimes. I heard him and Shelly recently got engaged, hopefully, she has enough sense to go ahead and marry him before they catch up to him. At least she'll get to keep his stash money when they do.

I haven't looked back since leaving Washington. Life is completely different now, for the best. Tia and Darius decided against staying there too; they've moved to Los Angeles instead. It fits both of their lifestyles and habits better. I'm happy they chose California because it gives me an excuse to visit often. Rocky even moved. I offered her a job managing my food trucks. After I saw they had released Gabe from prison and closed the bar after Gabriel went on the run, I felt it my duty to look out for her. Ryan would appreciate it.

She accepted the position and moved here a month later. She has been such a great help; I don't know how I'd manage without her. Xay and I stay so busy; if it weren't for her picking up my slack, I wouldn't be able to live out my dream. Xay has been the force behind a lot of the recent popular apps–He built majority of their interfaces. They have proven to drive customer satisfaction which led him to make a business out of it. I couldn't be more proud of him. He's doing what he loves every day now. To see him happy in every aspect of life makes me feel like we finally made it through the trenches.

When we first moved to Colorado, I was in search for a new therapist, the ones Dr. Rainey knew were too far away from me. I initially decided I could handle it without therapy. Dr. Rainey was persistent in reaching out, urging me not to take a break. She believed and still does believe that I am in a fragile state; possibly on the verge of creating another alter. She scared me by telling me something about our last session that I have no recollection of, but it was after we had already switched. I didn't and still don't have memories of another alter, I can only feel Koni.

I've decided to continue my sessions with her by phone instead, at least until I'm able to find a suitable replacement. During one of our phone sessions, she suggested that I share my story with one of her patients that she believed was going through a similar battle with self. I've gotten to a pretty decent space in sharing my body with someone that I don't identify as myself. I initially declined her suggestion. She offered me significant compensation, which is more than what my businesses were making until recently. Since then, I've been going around to different mental health conventions and sharing my experience living with DID, making good money doing so too.

The journey has taught me so much; I now feel it is my duty to share my story. To show that if I can be phenomenally successful and functional–even when it's made harder by sharing space with an alter, it's possible for so many others like me. The amount of people I've met with similar stories to my own since becoming a speaker is mind-blowing. Most of them are just like me. They live a regular life, and nothing seems out of the ordinary until something, usually a traumatic event, brings an alter out, and they begin to question their entire lives. It's nice to be able to help others through such a hard and confusing time. It's good to be able to show and prove that there is nothing wrong with us, that we can be successful and, most importantly, happy, too.

Once Xay and I leave the courthouse, it'll be one more major life goal conquered. It's so good to have found someone who loves us both. I'm surprised I haven't heard from Ryan today. She always seems to be tuned in when anything of significance happens. She'll be happy to discover what's about to happen when she finally does tune in. We're about to get married; Congratulations are in order for us both.

I'm trying my hardest to hide what I'm thinking; I don't want Koni to overhear. I don't want to ruin her happily ever after shit, but Xay was right. I told him I am anti-marriage because I didn't want him to come with any shit like this. I had a feeling it was coming; I was hoping that I was wrong. Xay is a good man and all, but I miss being able to have something new. Having new people spoil me, being able to manipulate multiple people at the same time; it's always boosted my ego. I really get off on it, I never knew how much until it was gone.

I miss fucking. I mean nasty, "I don't know, let alone care, what your name is fucking," it's something about it that fulfills me differently. I also miss looking down and getting to see my pussy on the pretty face of a woman. Xay is still nasty and great in bed, but I no longer believe I'm the marriage type. I've gotten bored even with someone as amazing as Xay. How does that even happen? The compromise we have going works more in Koni's favor. I get more nights than her, but they're all spent fucking Xay. Since we live together, it's not as easy to do what I'd like to do without having to answer to a motherfucker. I'm starting to get frustrated.

It's supposed to be my night in a few hours, but I have to crash this party. I'm trying to get my thoughts together. I actually care about Xay and don't want to hurt his feelings by declining. But if I don't tell them now, I'll be the first to cheat and hurt us all in other ways. When did I start giving a fuck about others? It's truly sickening. I miss the conflict that I used to get myself into; the tough and dangerous situations I had to work myself out of. I prefer everything not being so damn predictable. Granted, right now, we have a lot going on collectively. With the conventions and constantly interacting with others, it just makes me crave the first two free years alone back. We're rich in most ways, but I feel as if I'm starving; it's like I'm locked up all over again.

We pull up to the courthouse. Xay looks over at me. He reaches in his pocket and pulls out a black box with the same emblem as Gabriel has. I don't recall him having a jewelry business; I wonder what that's about. He turns to me and flashes the biggest smile.

"Baby are you sure you're ready?" he asks. Sweat begins to gather at the bridge of his nose.

"No. No, I am not," I look over at him, then look away quickly, feeling the tears emerging. "I can't look at you. I don't want to marry you. I'm not ready. If you go through with it anyway, you two will pray you listened the first time," I say, swiping my face quickly to catch the tears before they fall.

I watch as he slides the box back in his pocket. I feel Koni trying to force herself out. I focus on the anger I'd feel if I had to continue life as is. I focus so much everything begins to go blank, I can't hear or feel her anymore. I also can't see or hear Xay.

"Ry? I thought you wanted this forever, too," he says as he stares out the window. After several minutes of silence, he turns to look at me.

"Ry? Are you straight?" He waves his hand in my face.

"What are you calling me? Ry? That's a boy's name." the childlike voice giggles. "Who are you?"

Acknowledgments

I have so many stories inside of me. They've always been here. When I was younger, I was one of those avid diary girls. Fun fact, I've kept one since second grade. I began writing stories in fourth grade and letting others read by sixth. At the time, it was typical fan fiction. My personal favorite to write about was Lil Bow Wow.

Even back then, the stories were doing the most. I'm laughing, thinking back on how much drama I wrote. My friends, as well as their friends, were reading and requesting more. I've written on and off throughout the years. In high school, I swore I was the next Zane. Again, I'm laughing at myself. However, the short stories were fire. So fire, people stole everyone I wrote. I wish I still had them to reflect on to compare my growth. Here's to starting a new, improved collection.

This book came from promises I made to myself. Sometimes you have to prove to yourself that you can and will do all the things you set out to. I finally got started. I felt I owed this to myself. Writing is my forever love. It also serves as therapy, which is why I chose to focus on mental health in this book. Getting back to the things I am passionate about helps me keep peace within myself. I wanted to display the internal battle that isn't immediately identifiable on the surface.

Please know this is only the beginning. Thank you to everyone who believed in me, who encouraged me, who even simply entertained me. Special shoutout to:

To Mom, you have a talent for writing, so thanks for unknowingly passing it to me. Without you there would be no me. I love you.

To my MAIN, Reem, thank you for being here every word of the way. You were the first to read from beginning to end, through even the roughest of drafts. Thank you for letting me bounce it all off of you.

To Essmora for inspiring me to continue to write. Seeing you make your dreams possible gave me additional motivation. You've helped and encouraged me so much, I'm forever thankful.

To my sister, Ilysha. You are the biggest non avid reader supporter! From gifting me with a major key in my publishing journey to the constant reminder of how much you believe in me. The support is always unreal. I love you Dirty Dan.

To my Illustrator and sister, Will Nika Draw, thank you for your patience throughout this project and delivering superb quality with each draft. I know I drive you well past crazy. I love you Pinhead.

To my graphic designer, I have so much faith in you and your talent. I am amazed by it daily. You really came through. As long as you allow me, I'll always choose you.

Lastly, to my dedicated first draft readers, thank you for the support from the beginning & the positive feedback, as well as the critique. It often helped me through the next chapter. Also, to my final beta readers, thank you for not holding back and taking on the task. I am forever appreciative.

About the Author

R. Latice is a poet, writer and recently met her goal of becoming an author with her new novel, *Walking Contradiction*. She has been a lifelong writer who first began creating other worlds and characters in the fourth grade. When she is not writing she can be found in her hometown of Little Rock, AR spending time with her family, spoiling her mini Australian Shepherd, dancing off beat to a great playlist, or managing her publishing company, Ward's Publishing House LLC.

To stay connected and keep up with upcoming projects and events, follow her at:

Website: rlatice.com
Facebook: R.Latice
Instagram: @R.Latice
Twitter: @r_latice

Or for publishing needs including editing, website or blog content, cover design, ghostwriting, interior formatting, self-publishing consultation, and social media management feel free to reach out to allow Wards Publishing House to take your project to the next level.

Website: wardspublishinghouse.com
Email: wardspublishinghouse@gmail.com

Printed in the USA
CPSIA information can be obtained
at www.ICGtesting.com
LVHW091321301223
767739LV00005B/206

9 781735 055701